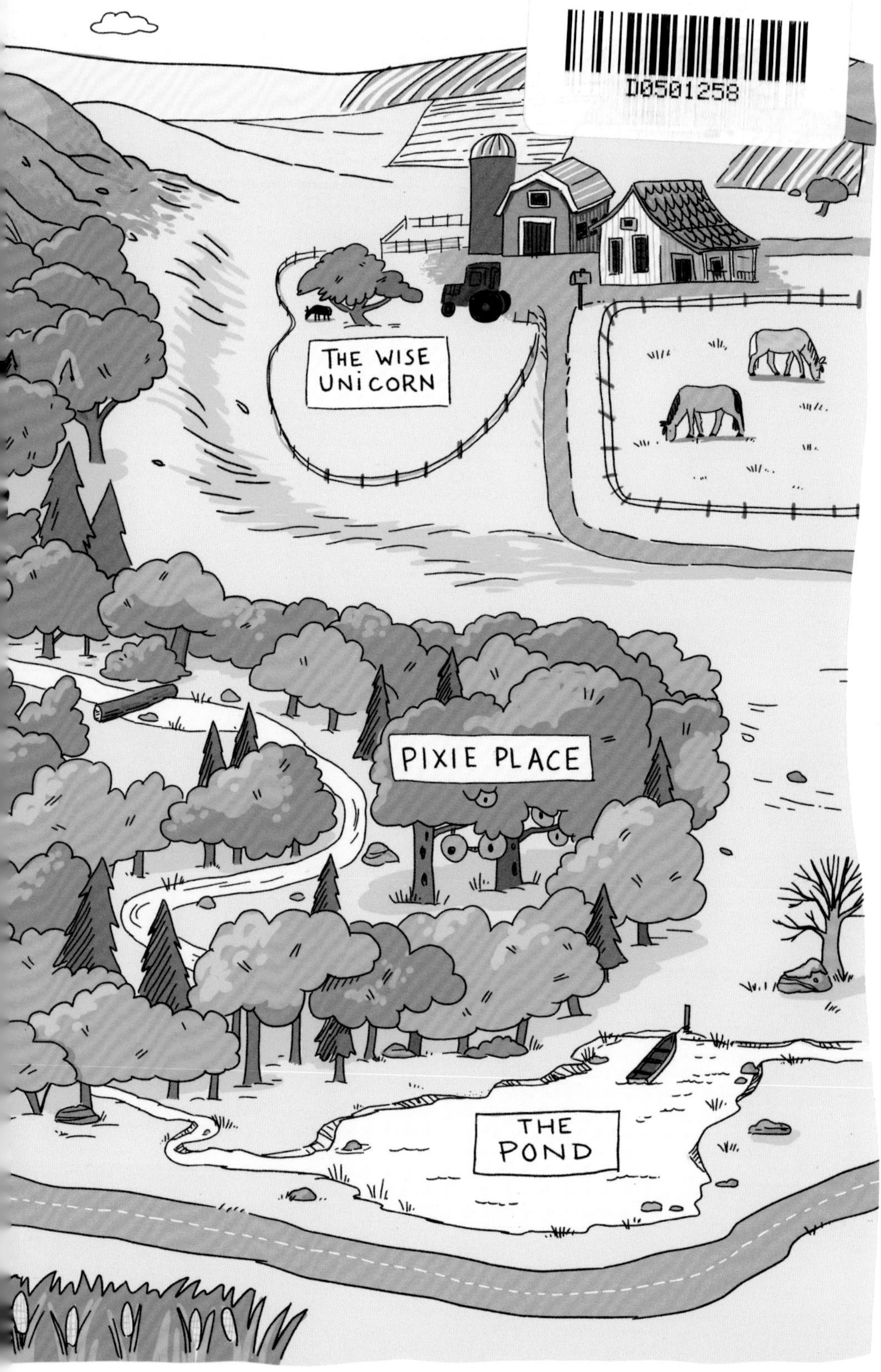
THE WISE UNICORN
PIXIE PLACE
THE POND

**I Like to Read® Comics instill confidence and the joy of reading in new readers. Created by award-winning artists as well as talented newcomers, these imaginative books support beginners' reading comprehension with extensive visual support.**

**We want to hear every new reader say, "I like to read comics!"**

---

**Visit our website for flash cards, activities, and more about the series:**
**www.holidayhouse.com/ILiketoRead**
**#ILTR**

## For the dynamic duo—Eelis and Aila

I LIKE TO READ is a registered trademark of Holiday House Publishing, Inc.


HOLIDAY HOUSE is registered in the U.S. Patent and Trademark Office.
Printed and bound in September 2022 at C&C Offset, Shenzhen, China.
The final art was created in Clip Studio Paint.
www.holidayhouse.com
First Edition
1 3 5 7 9 10 8 6 4 2

Library of Congress Cataloging-in-Publication Data

Names: Hokkanen, Mirka, author, illustrator.
Title: Mossy and Tweed : crazy for coconuts / Mirka Hokkanen.
Other titles: Crazy for coconuts
Description: First edition. | New York : Holiday House, 2023. | Series: I like to read comics
Audience: Ages 4-8. | Audience: Grades K-1. | Summary: "When a coconut lands near their homes, two clueless gnomes Mossy and Tweed think paradise could be inside and try to crack the coconut open" – Provided by publisher.
Identifiers: LCCN 2022022704 | ISBN 9780823452347 (hardcover)
Subjects: CYAC: Graphic novels. | Gnomes–Fiction. | Coconut–Fiction. | Humorous stories.
LCGFT: Humorous fiction. | Graphic novels.
Classification: LCC PZ7.7.H644 Mo 2023 | DDC 741.5/973–dc23/eng/20220719
LC record available at https://lccn.loc.gov/2022022704

ISBN: 978-0-8234-5234-7 (hardcover)

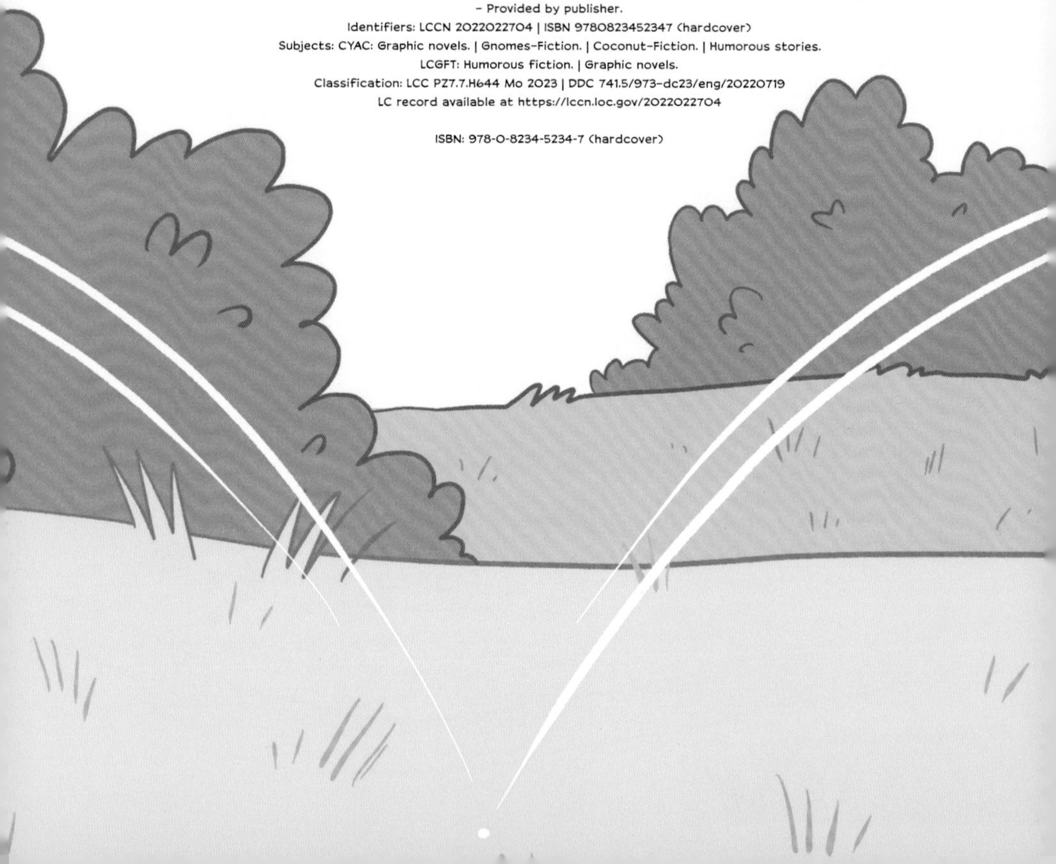

# MOSSY AND TWEED

## CRAZY FOR COCONUTS

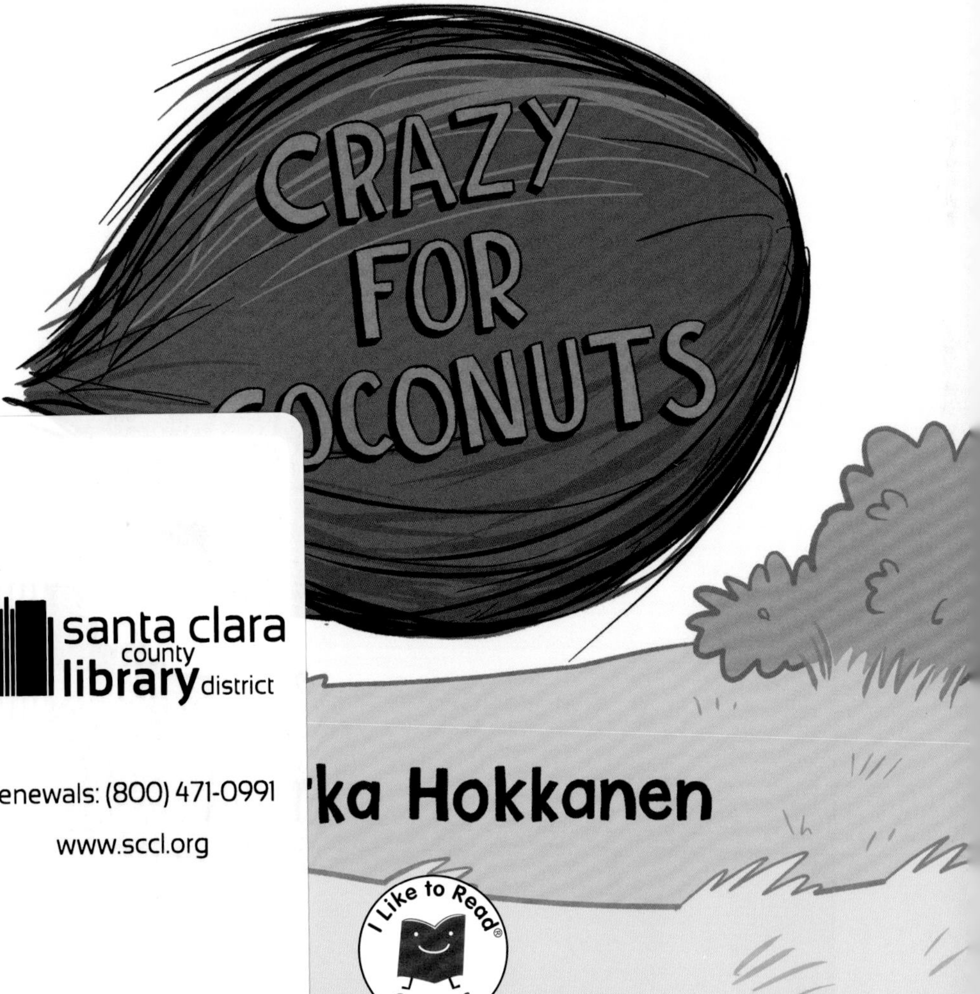



rka Hokkanen

I Like to Read® COMICS

HOLIDAY HOUSE • NEW YORK

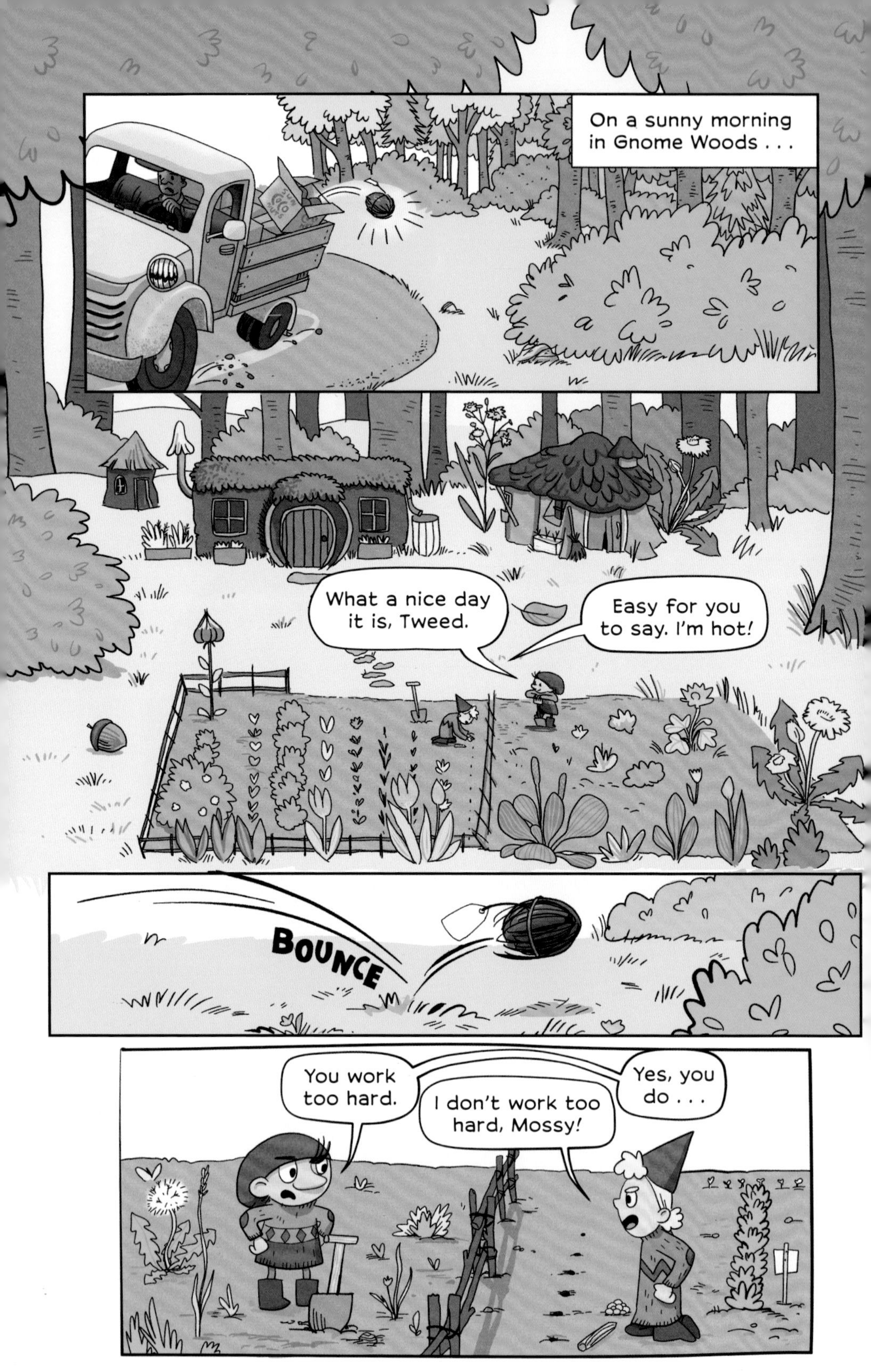
On a sunny morning in Gnome Woods . . .
What a nice day it is, Tweed.
Easy for you to say. I'm hot!
BOUNCE
You work too hard.
I don't work too hard, Mossy!
Yes, you do . . .

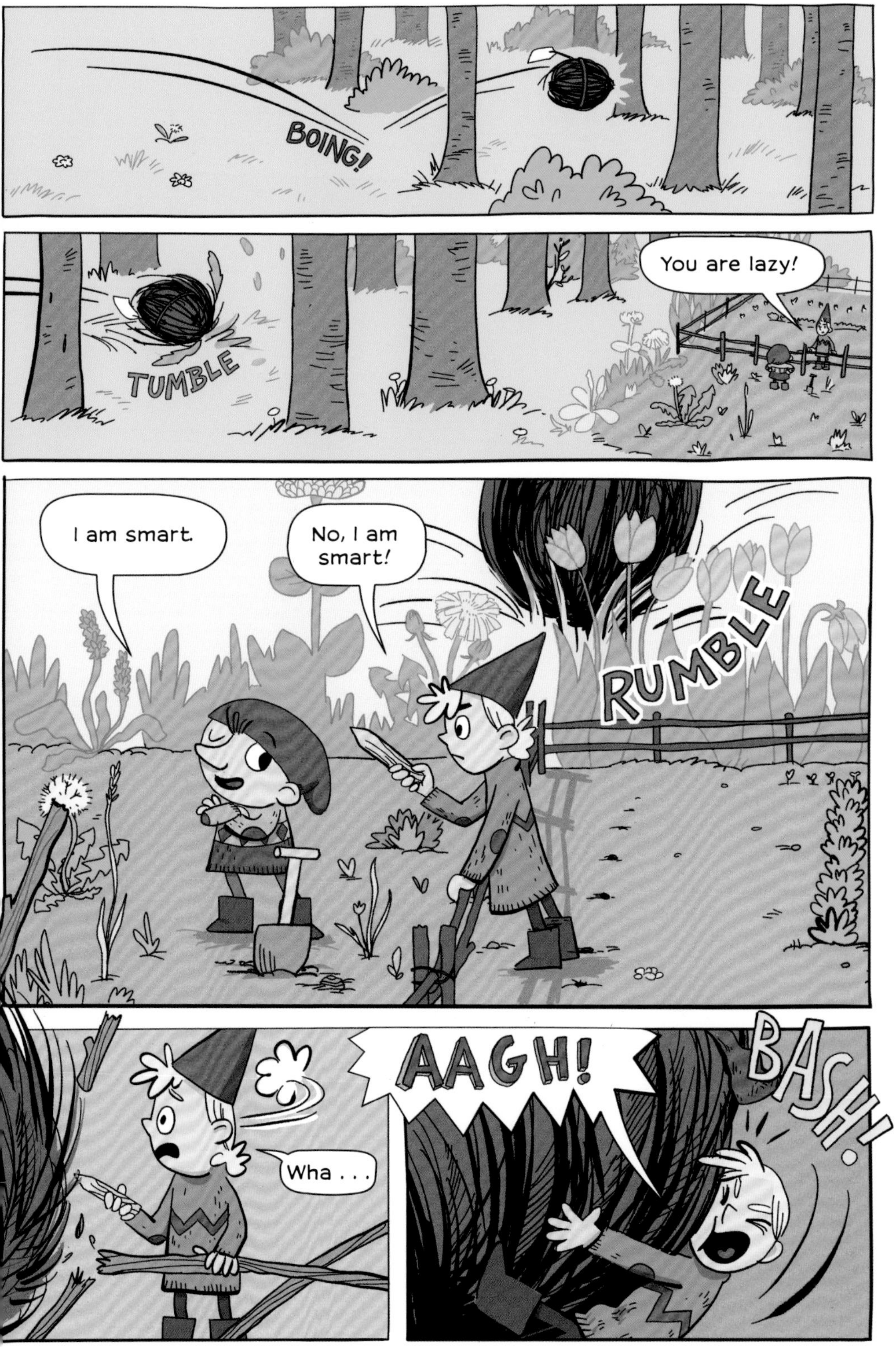
BOING!
TUMBLE
You are lazy!
I am smart.
No, I am smart!
RUMBLE
Wha . . .
AAGH!
BASH!

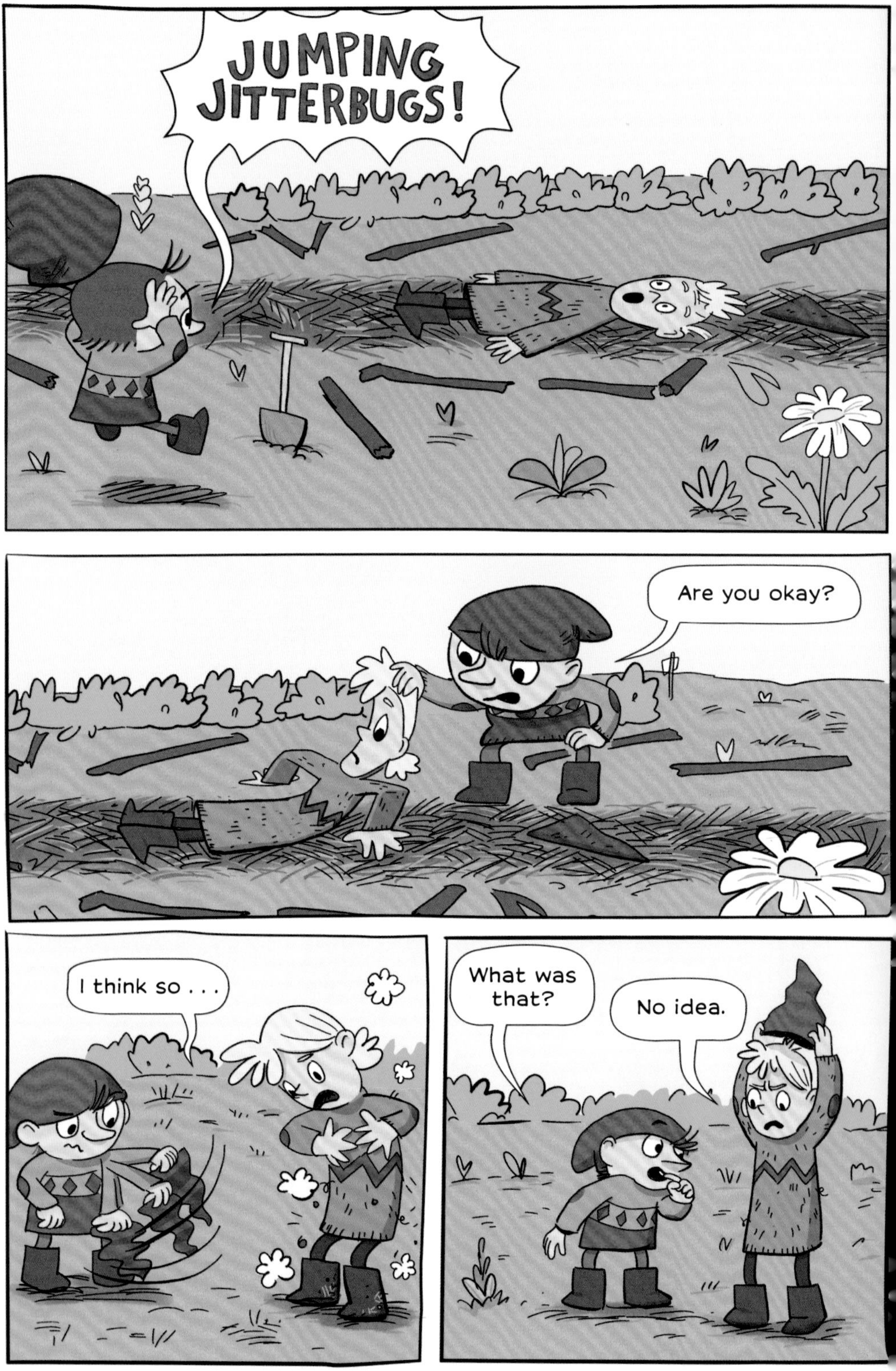
JUMPING JITTERBUGS!
Are you okay?
I think so . . .
What was that?
No idea.

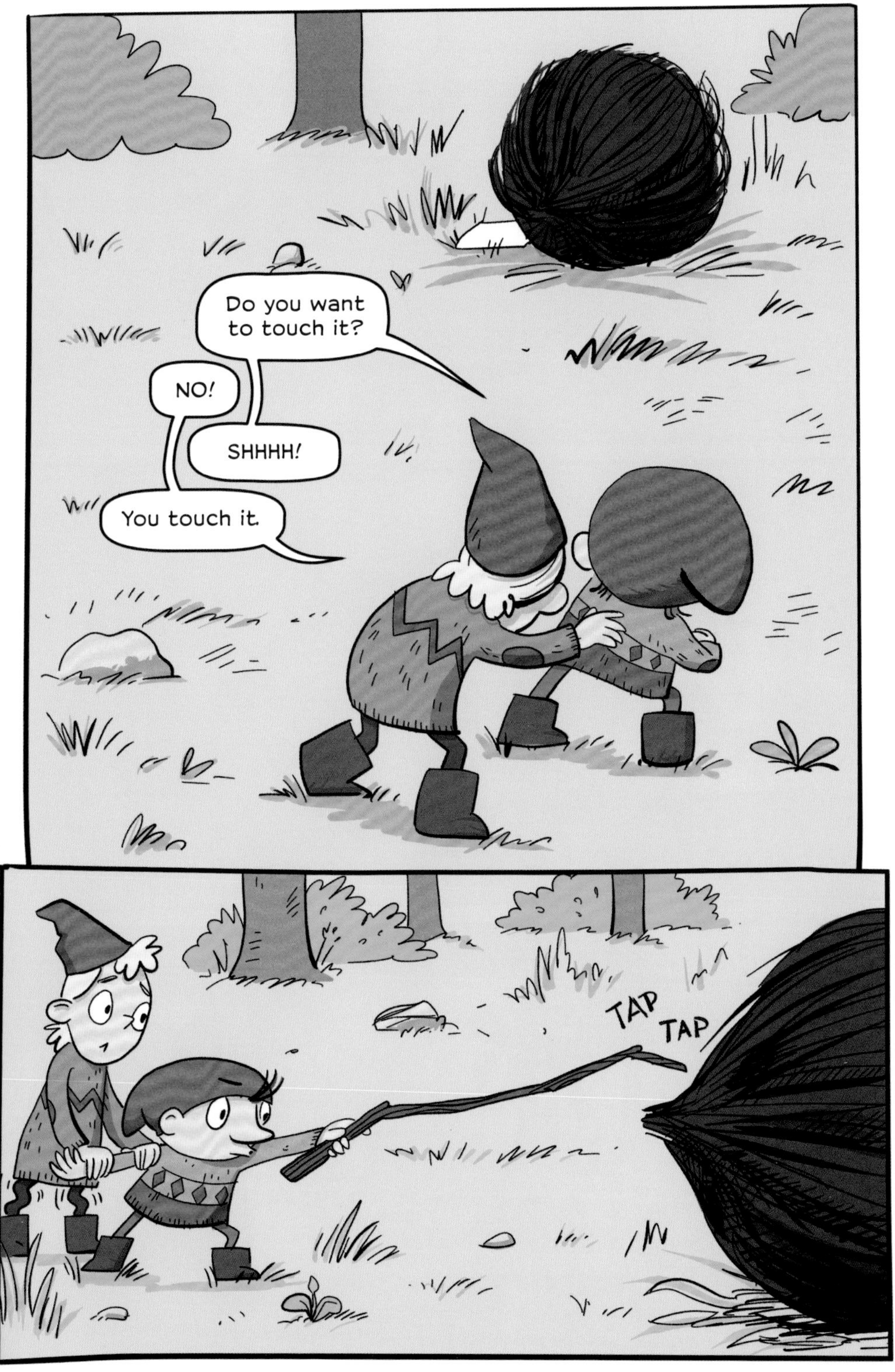
Do you want to touch it?
NO!
SHHHH!
You touch it.
TAP
TAP

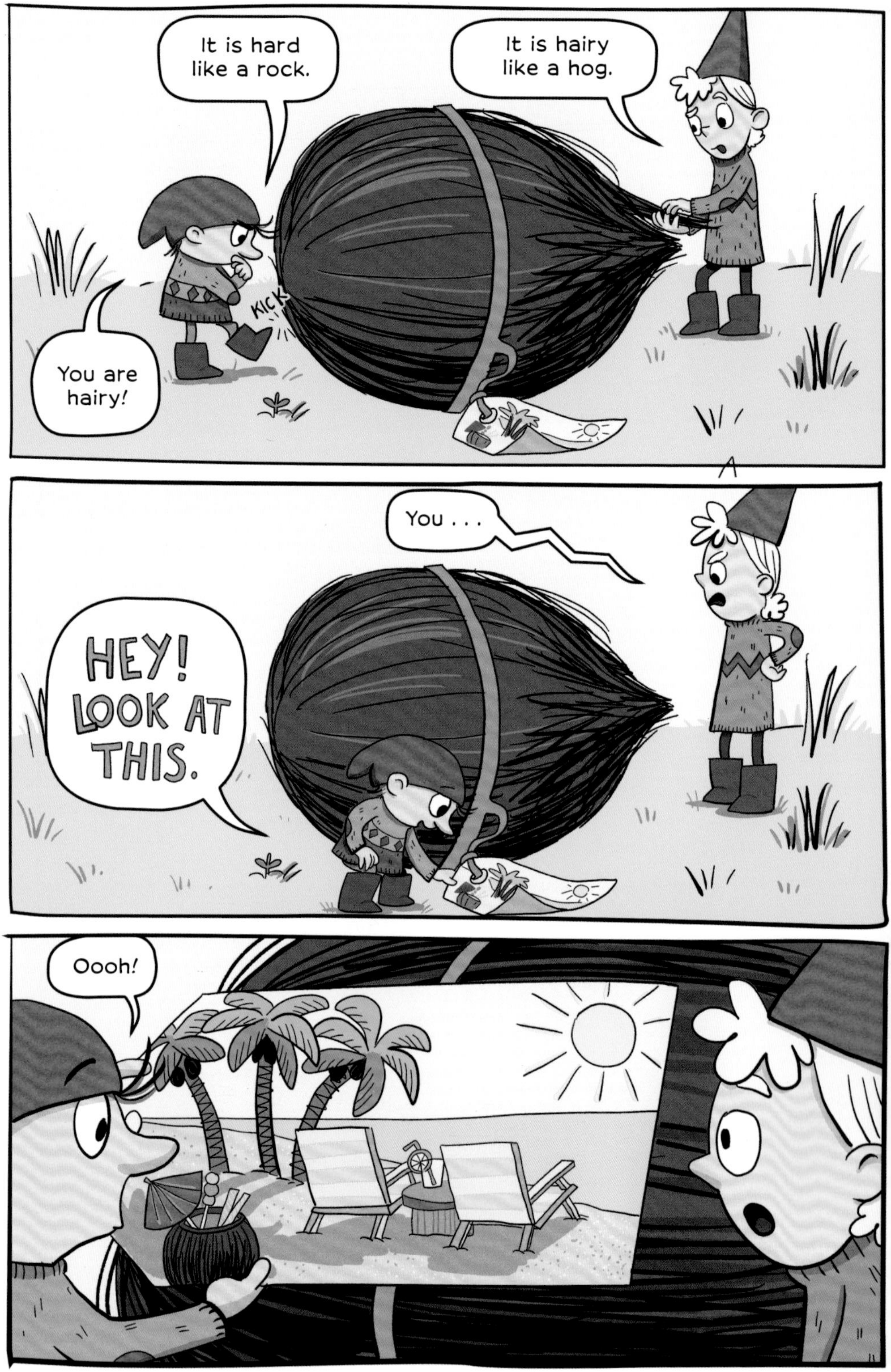
It is hard like a rock.
It is hairy like a hog.
KICK
You are hairy!
You . . .
HEY! LOOK AT THIS.
Oooh!

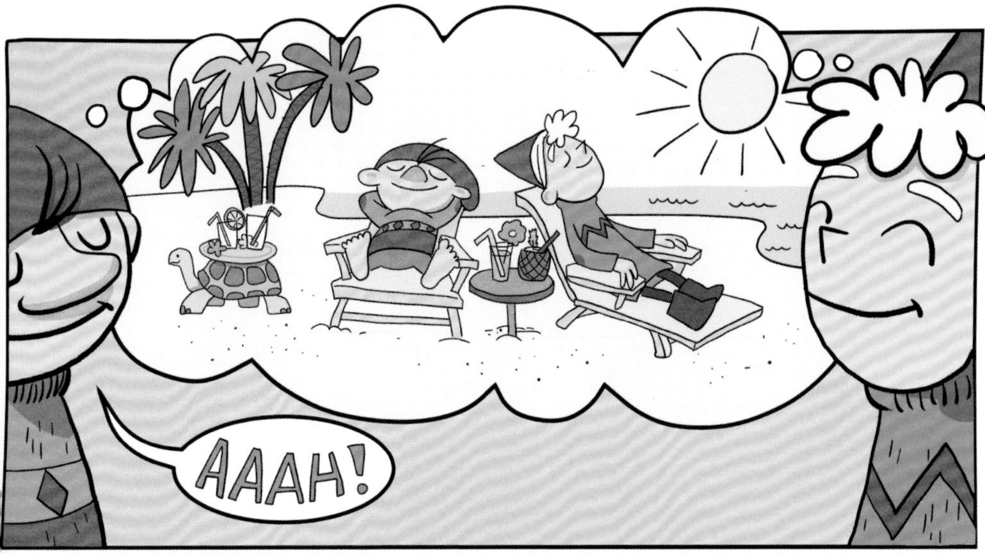
AAAH!

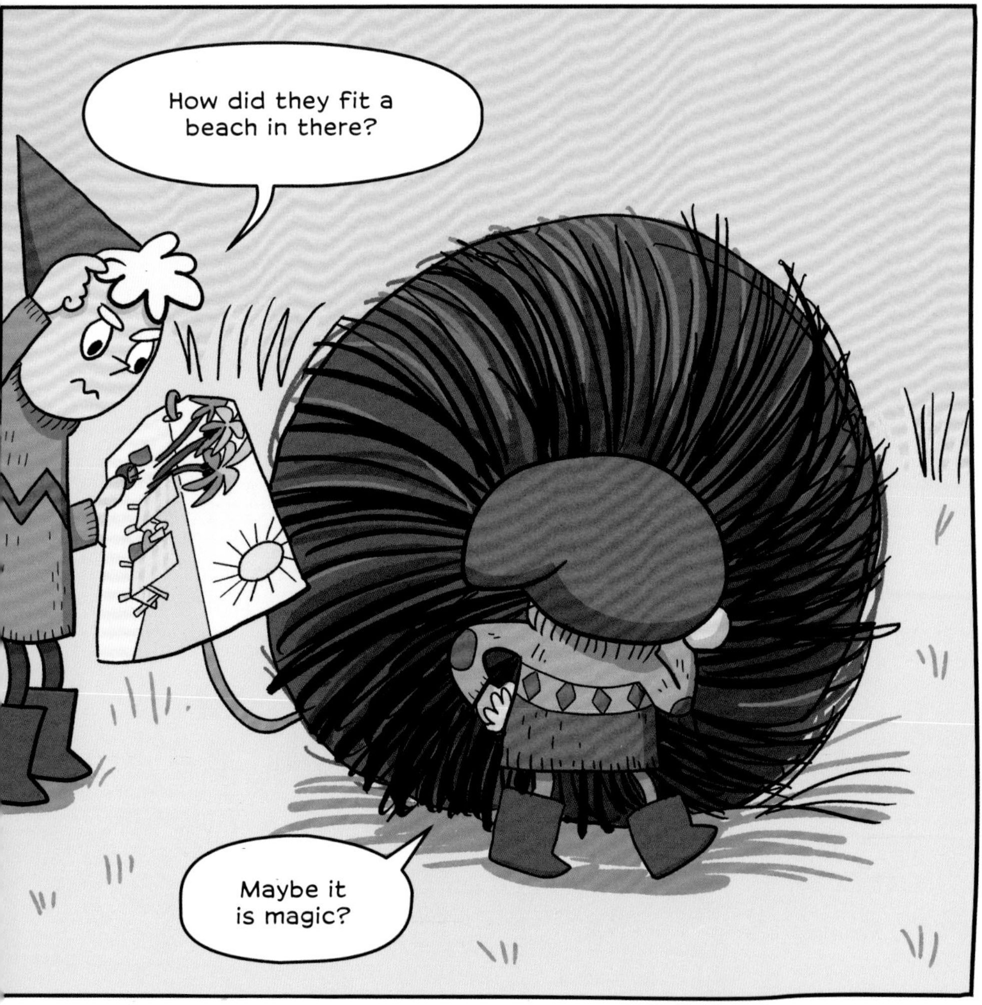
How did they fit a beach in there?
Maybe it is magic?

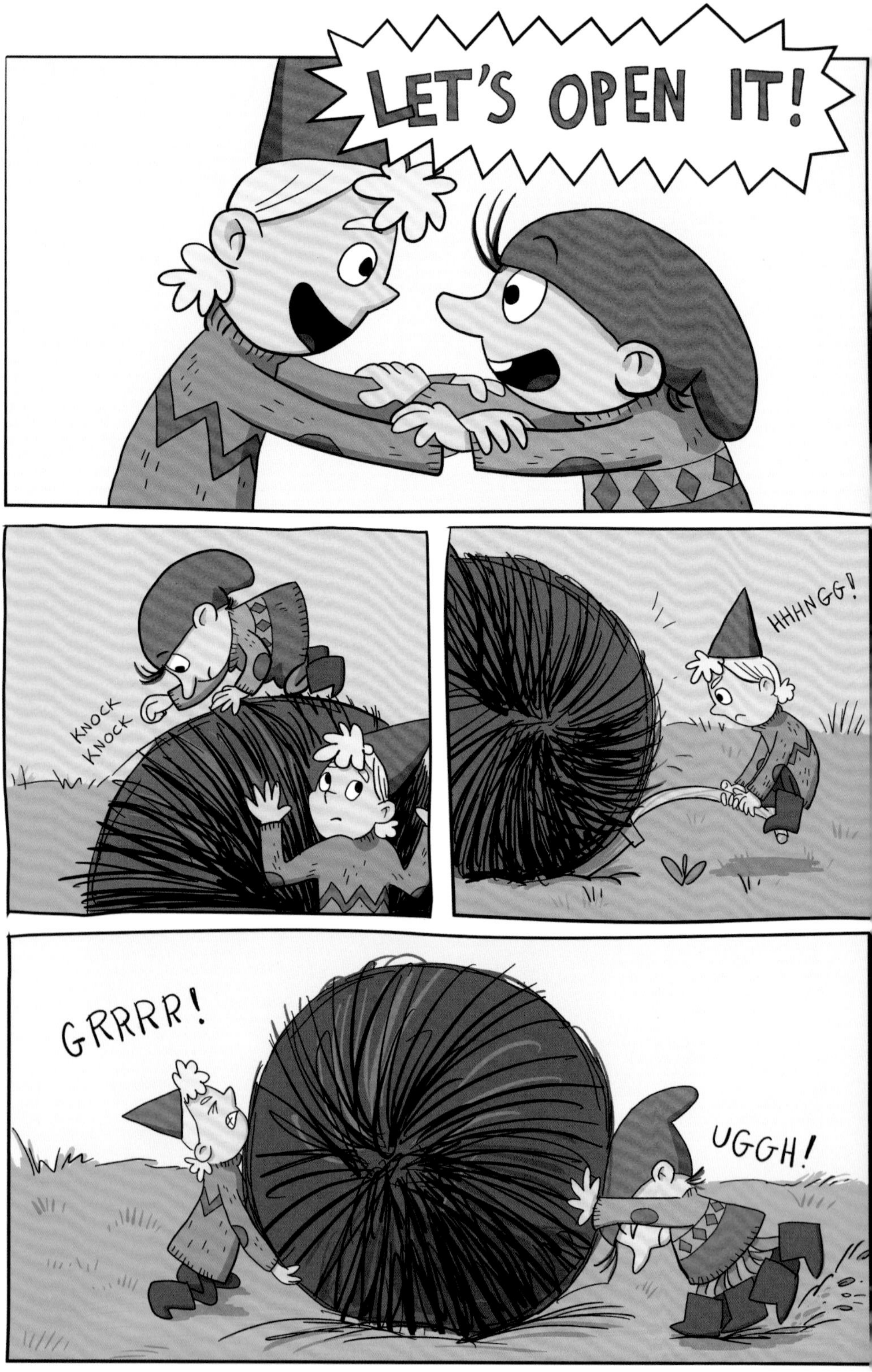
LET'S OPEN IT!
KNOCK KNOCK
HHHNGG!
GRRRR!
UGGH!

We can't do it.

Be right back.

Hmm.

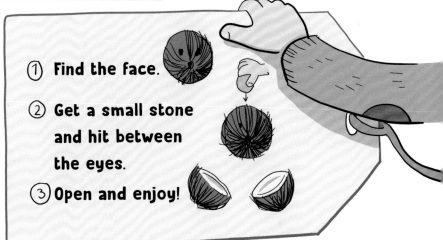

① **Find the face.**

② **Get a small stone and hit between the eyes.**

③ **Open and enjoy!**

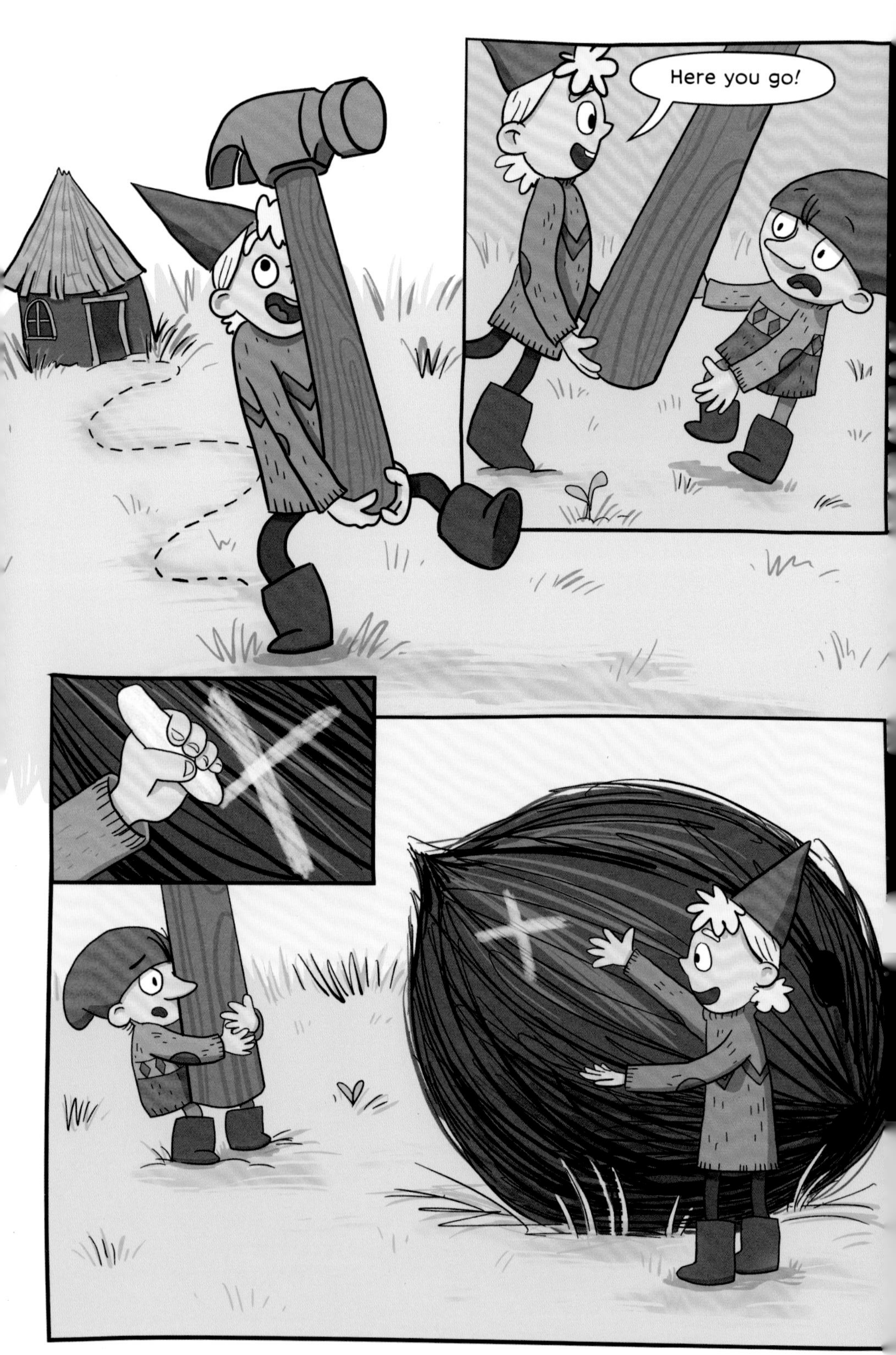
Here you go!

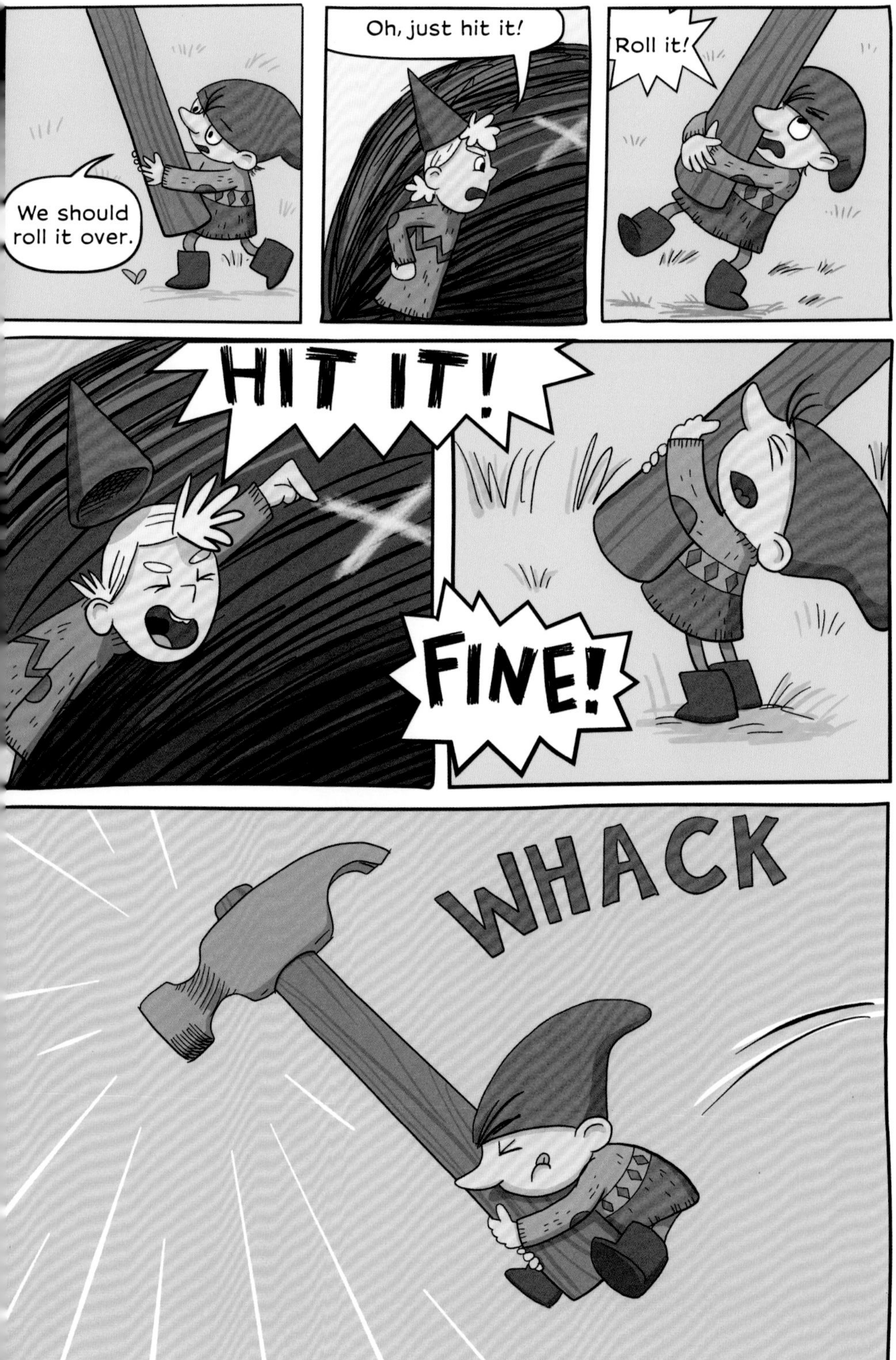
We should roll it over.
Oh, just hit it!
Roll it!
HIT IT!
FINE!
WHACK

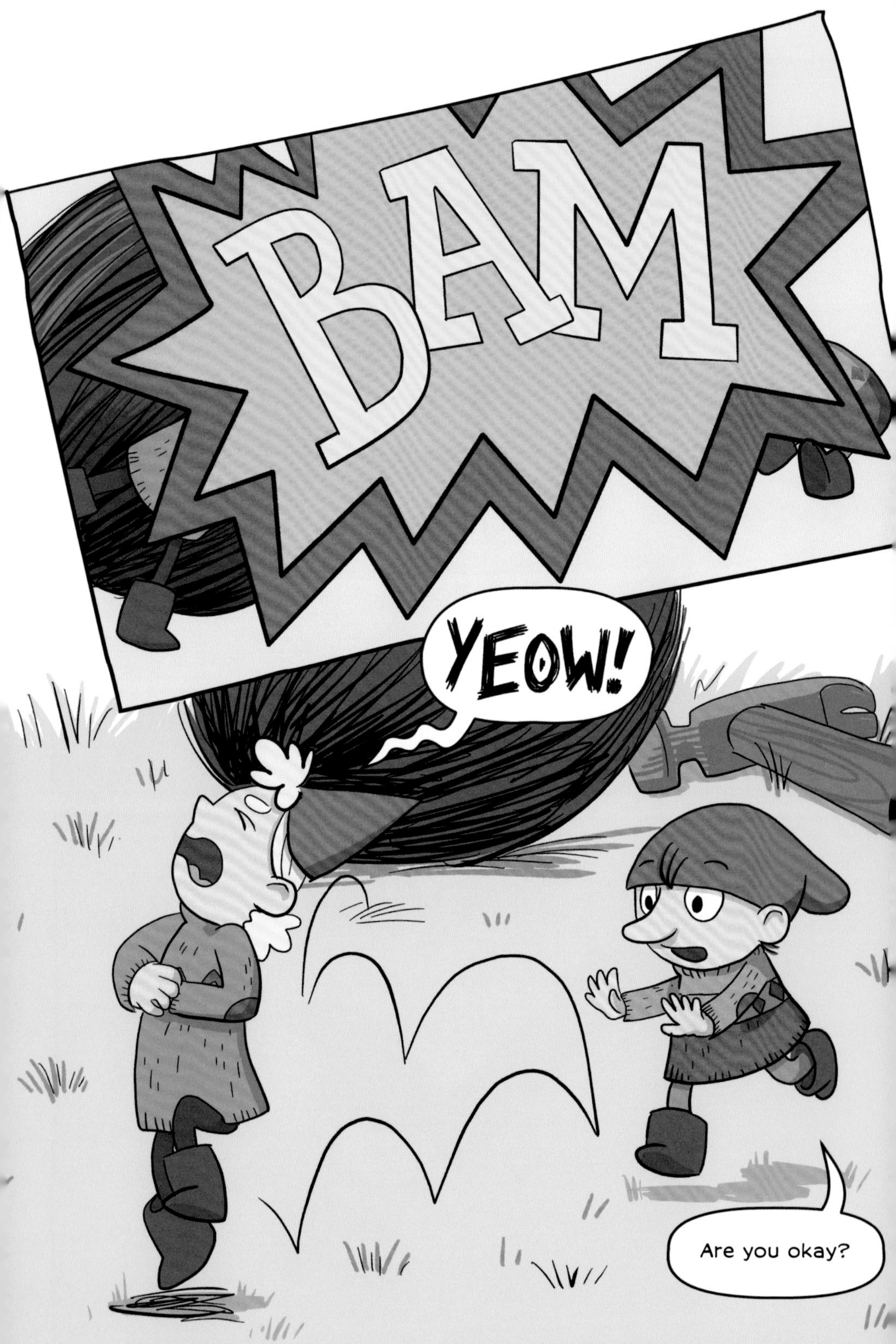
BAM
YEOW!
Are you okay?

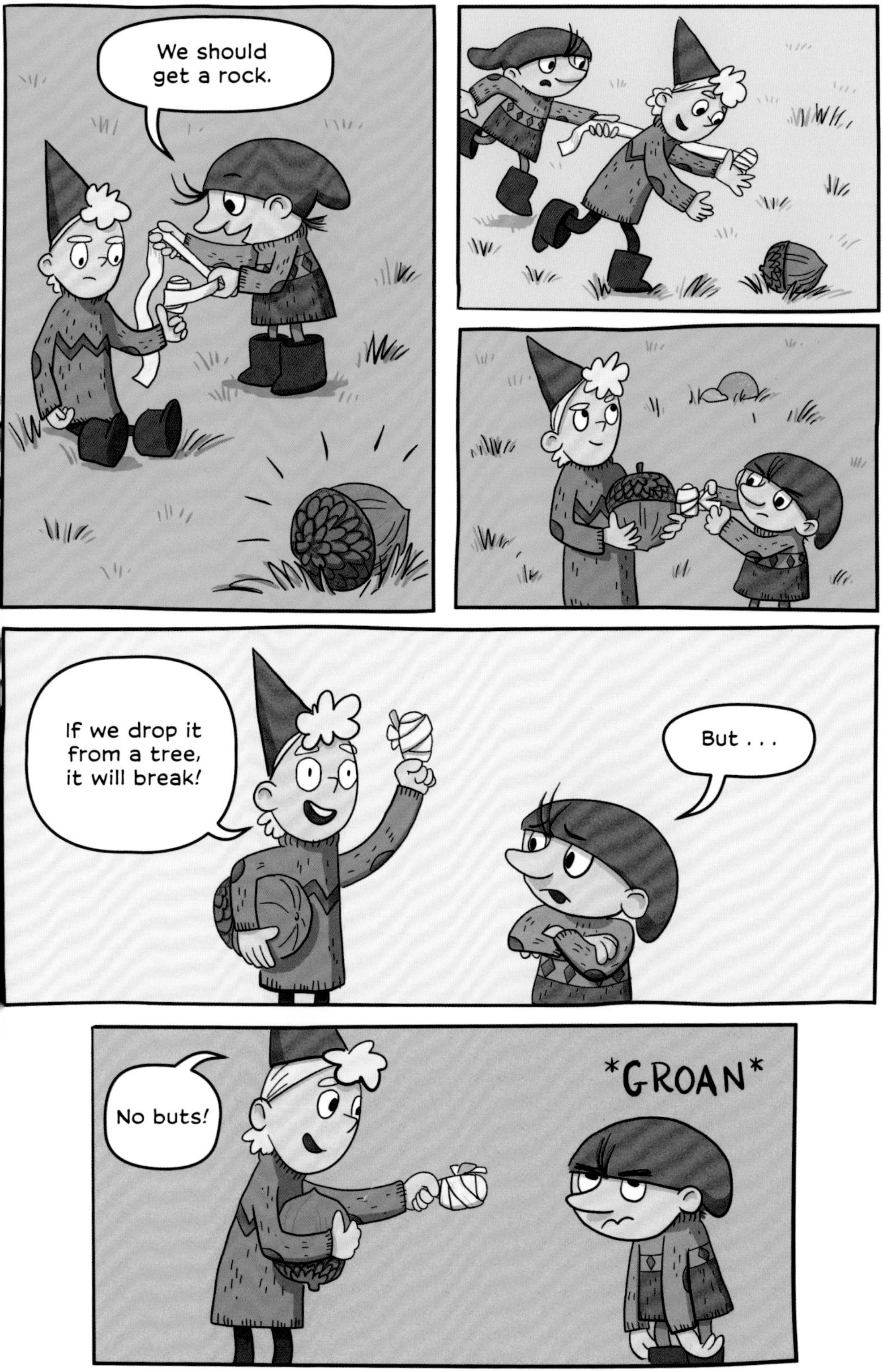
We should get a rock.
If we drop it from a tree, it will break!
But . . .
No buts!
*GROAN*

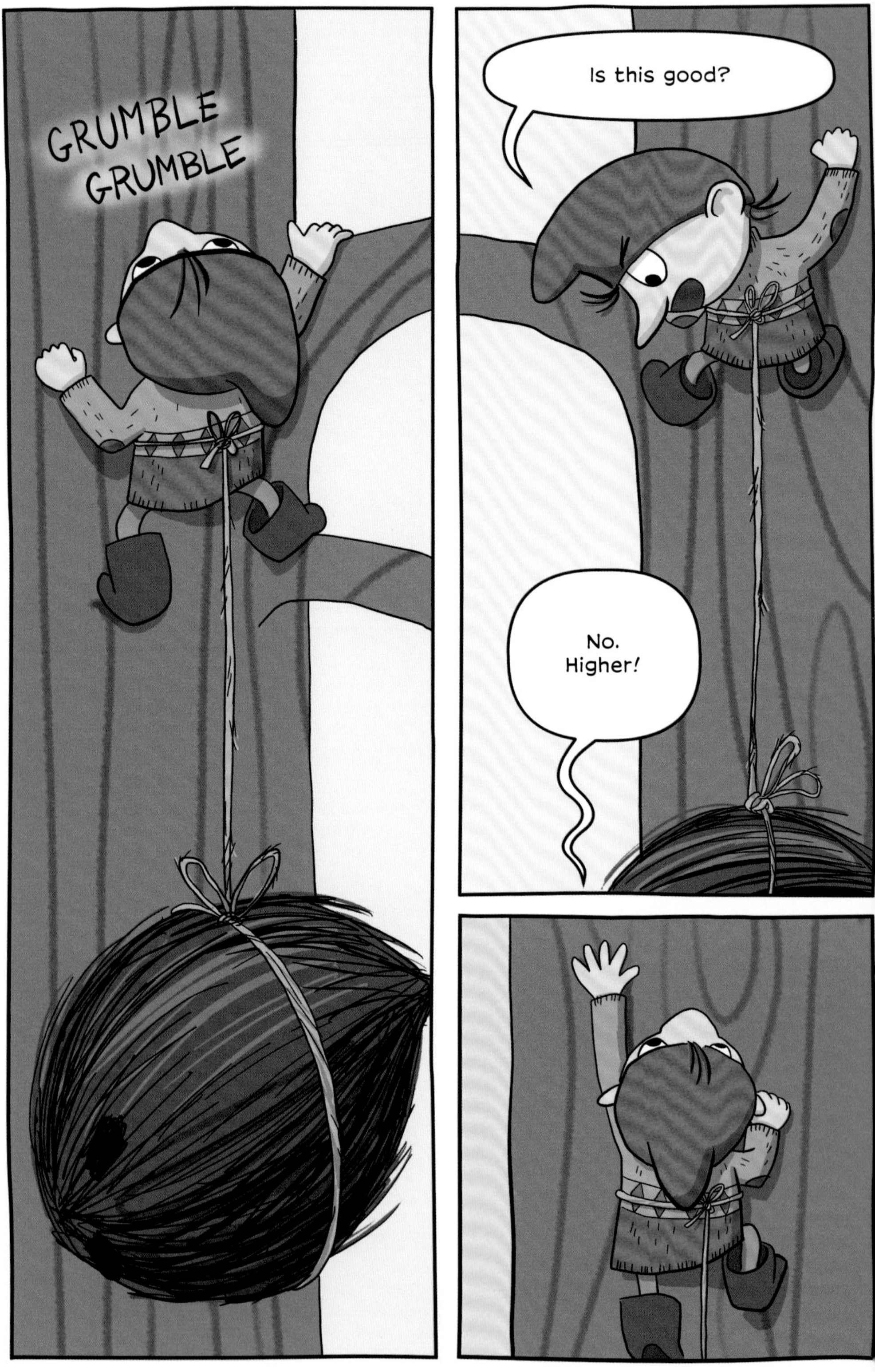
GRUMBLE
GRUMBLE
Is this good?
No. Higher!

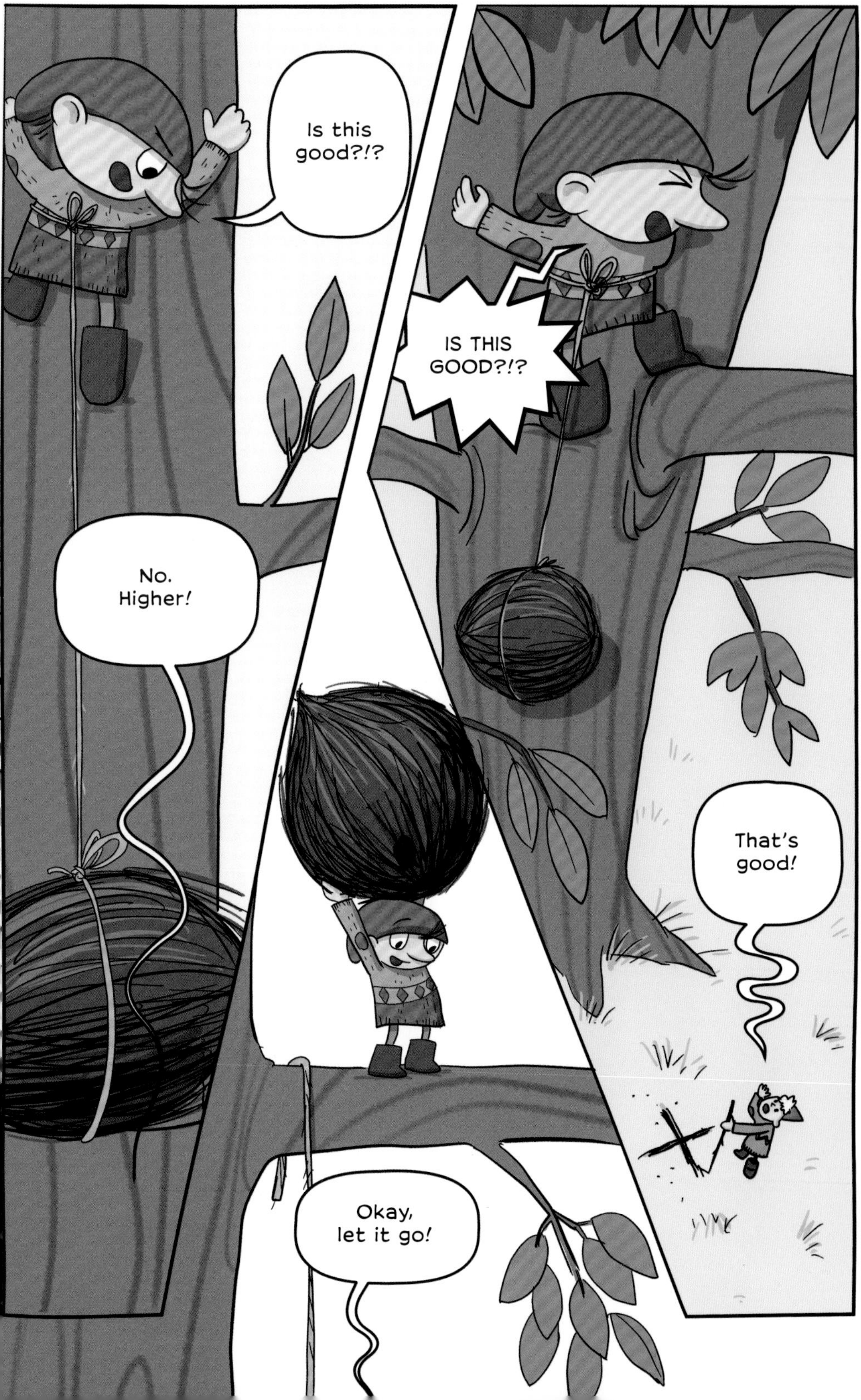
Is this good?!?
IS THIS GOOD?!?
No. Higher!
That's good!
Okay, let it go!

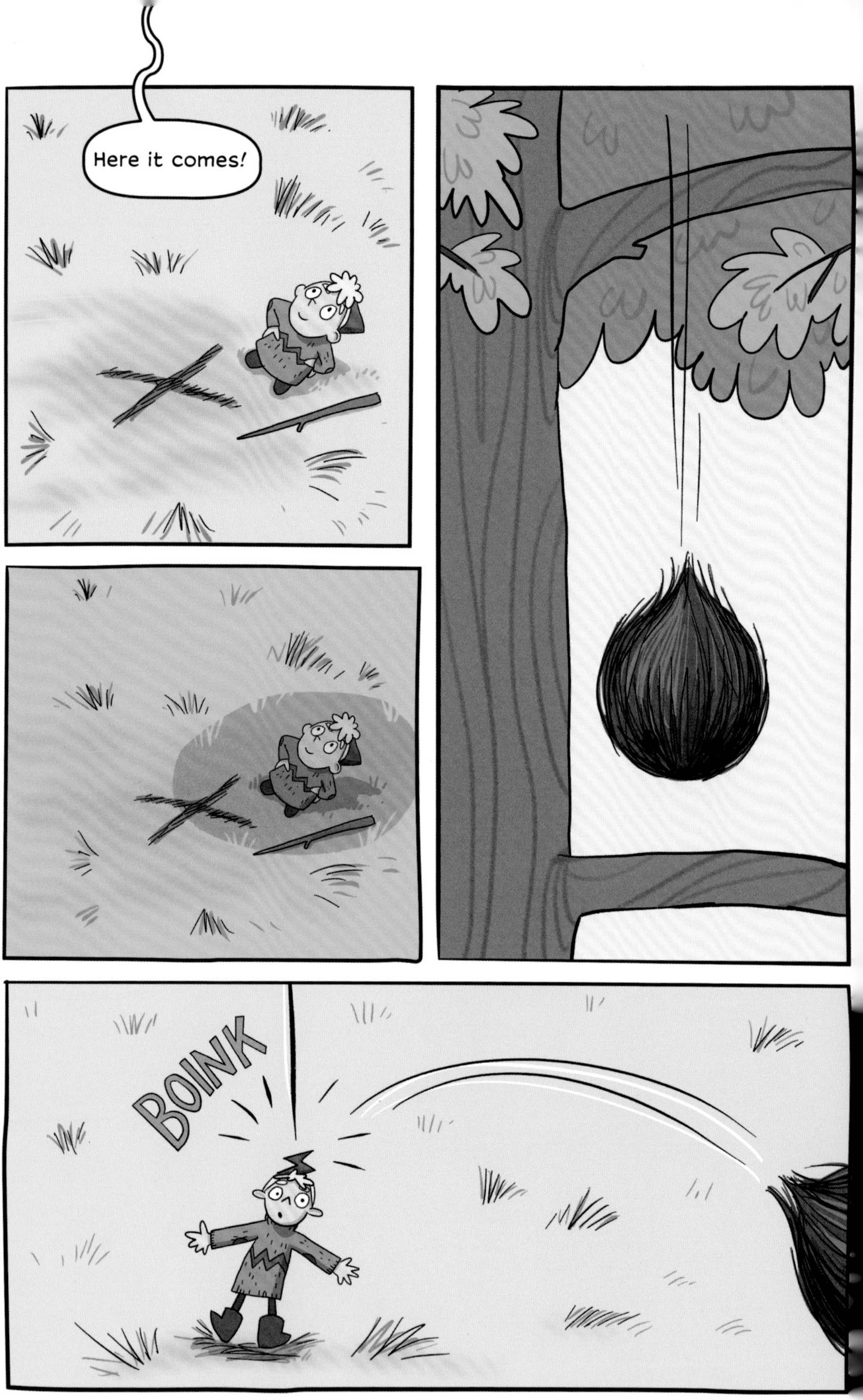
Here it comes!
BOINK

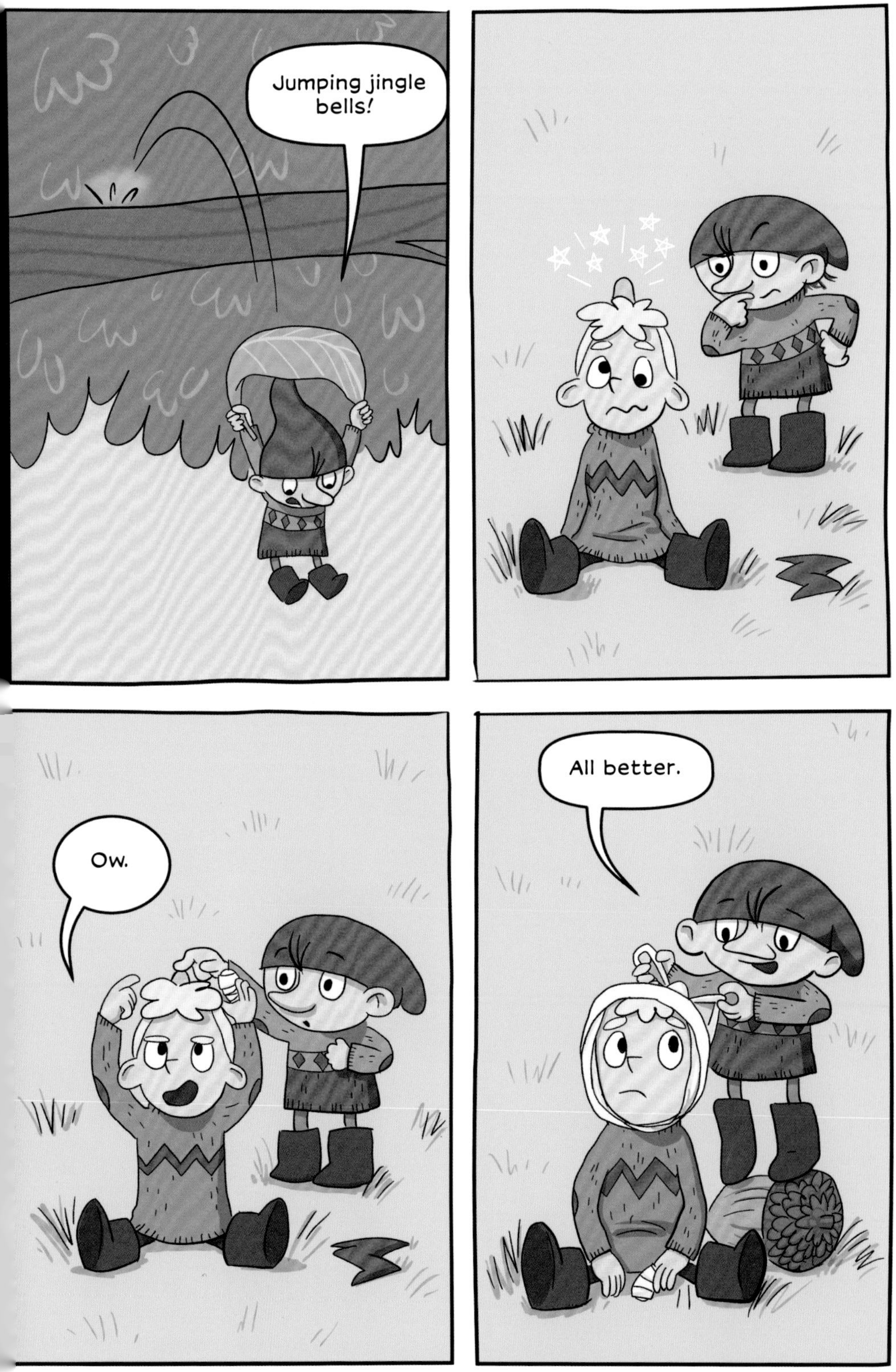
Jumping jingle bells!
Ow.
All better.

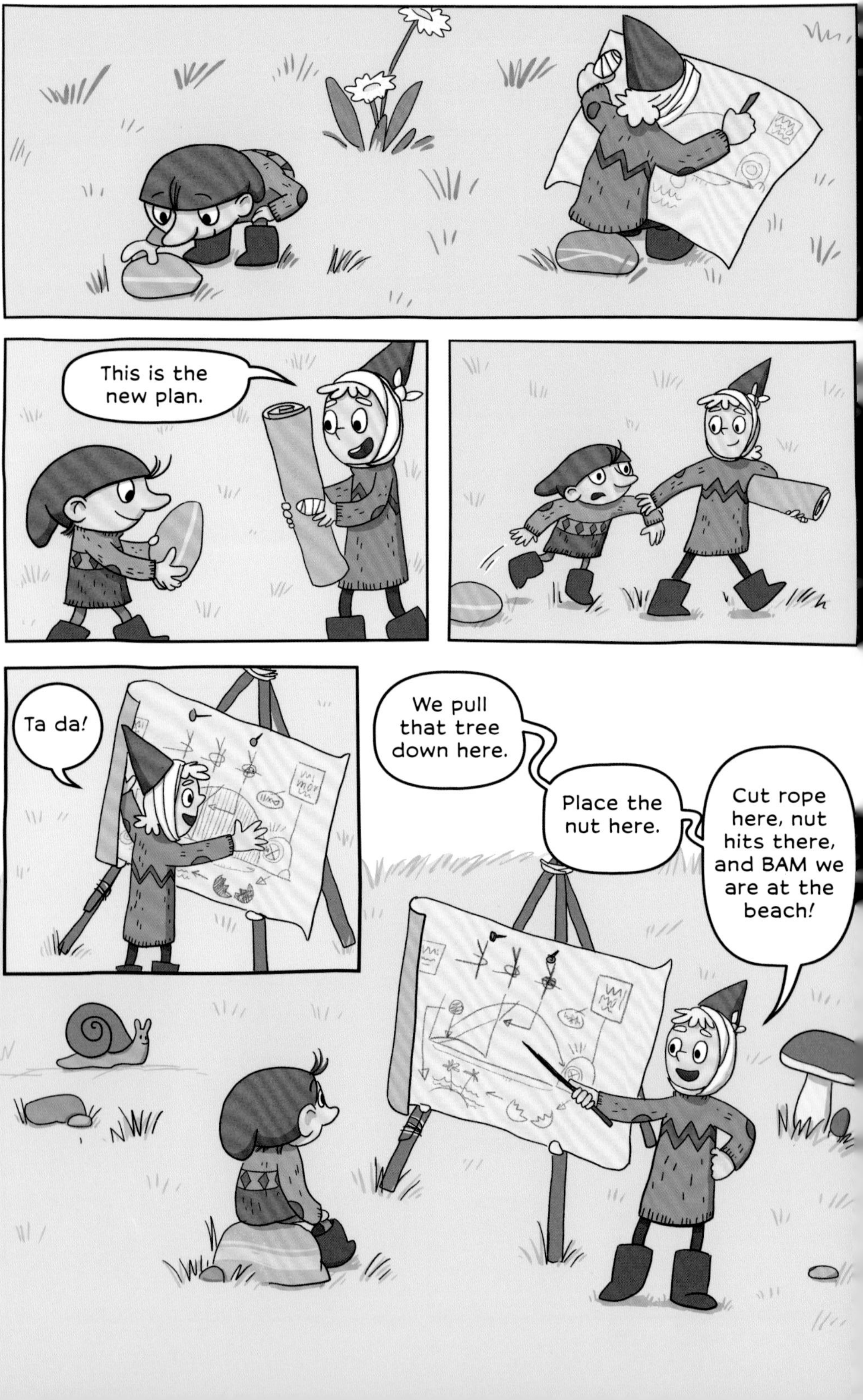
This is the new plan.
Ta da!
We pull that tree down here.
Place the nut here.
Cut rope here, nut hits there, and BAM we are at the beach!

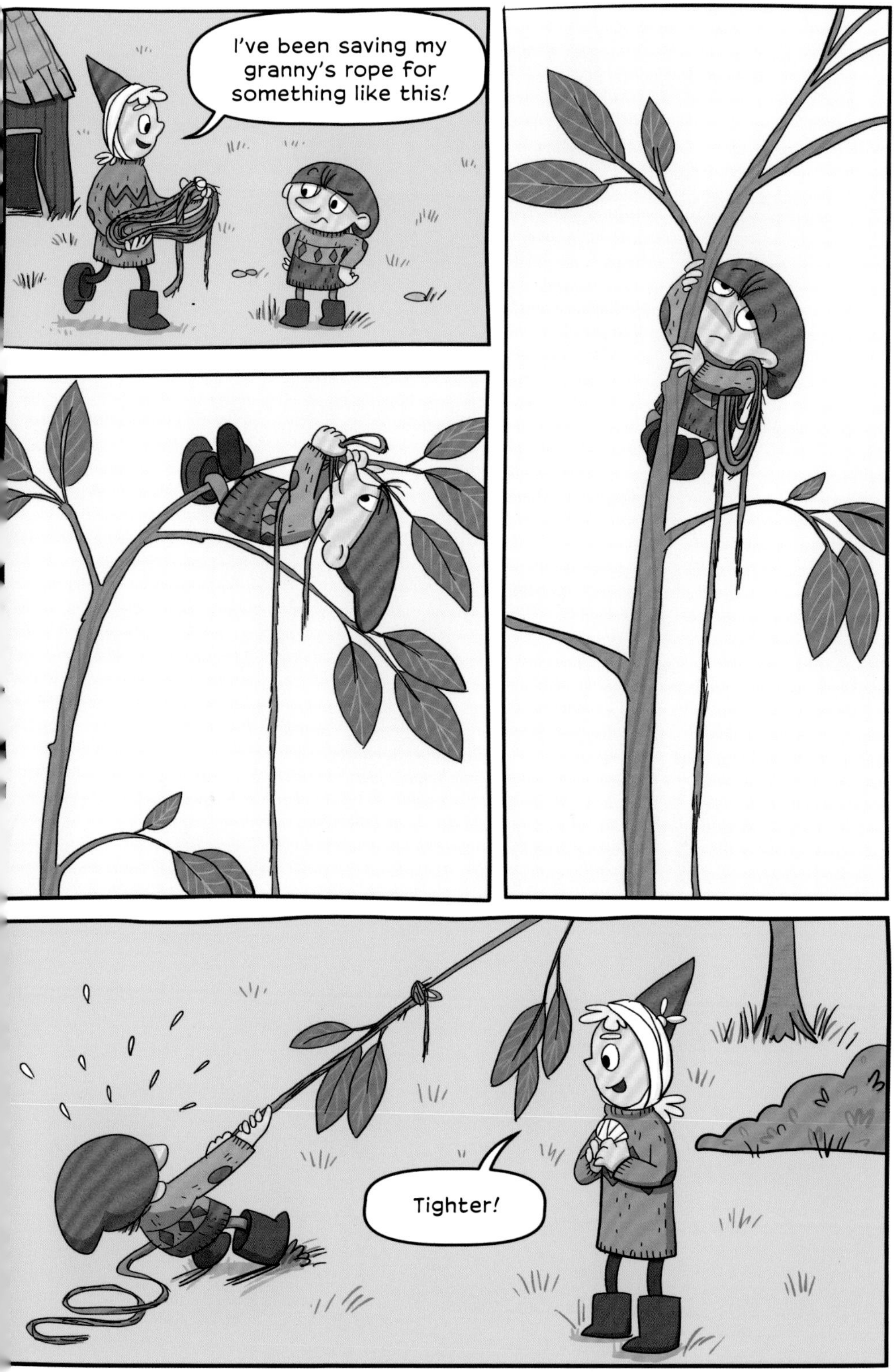
I've been saving my granny's rope for something like this!
Tighter!

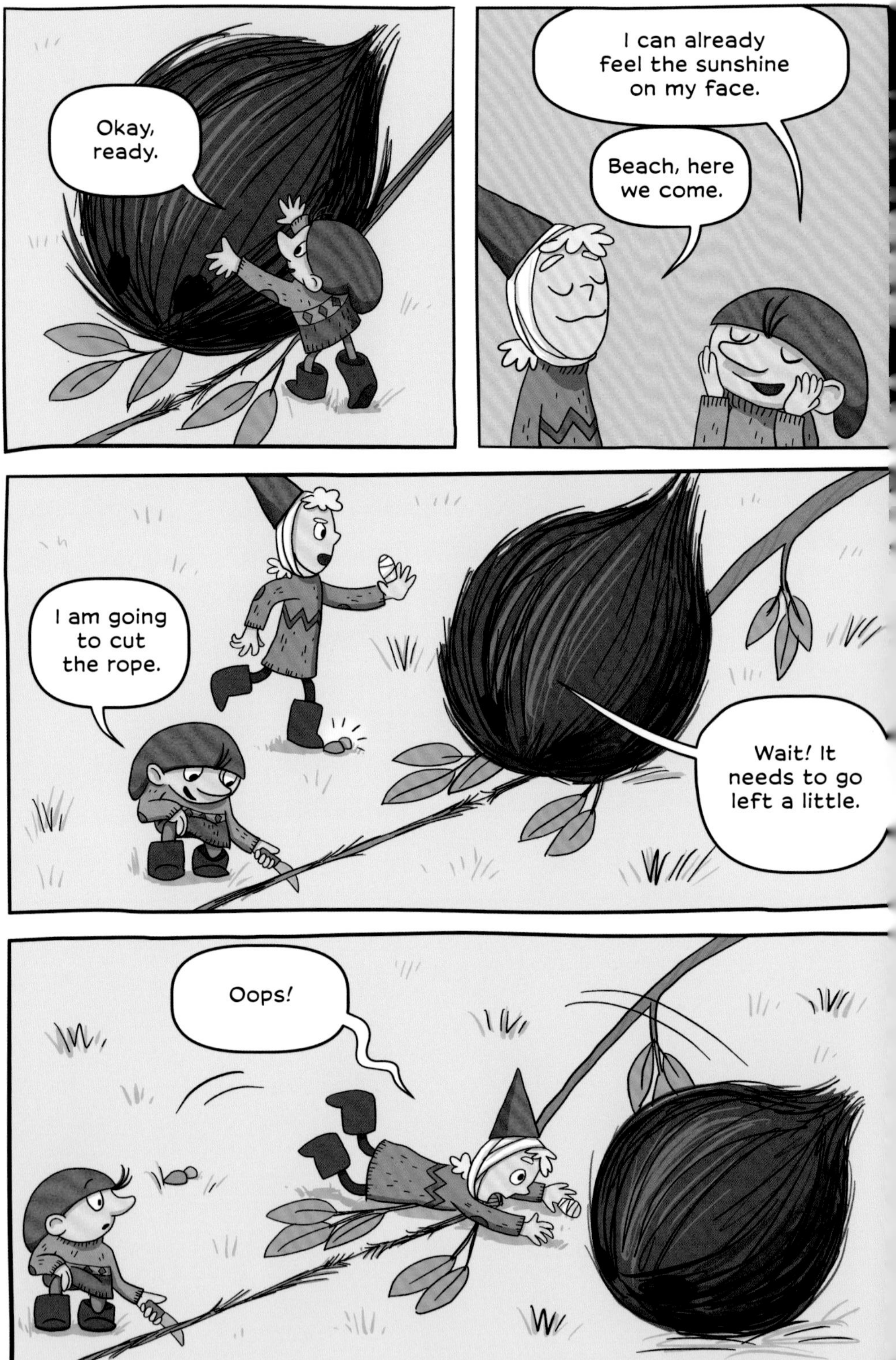
Okay, ready.
I can already feel the sunshine on my face.
Beach, here we come.
I am going to cut the rope.
Wait! It needs to go left a little.
Oops!

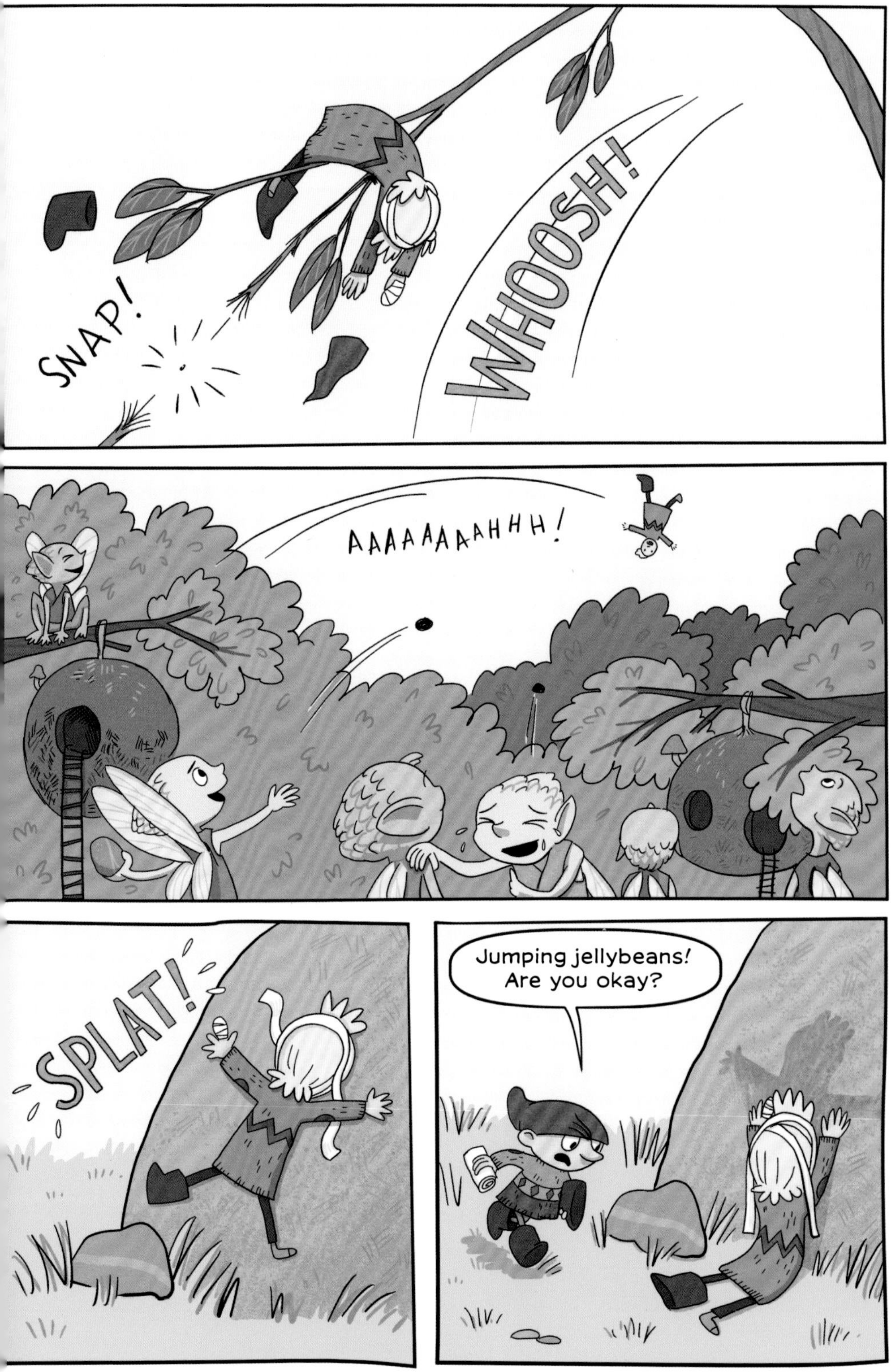
SNAP!
WHOOSH!
AAAAAAAAHHH!
SPLAT!
Jumping jellybeans!
Are you okay?

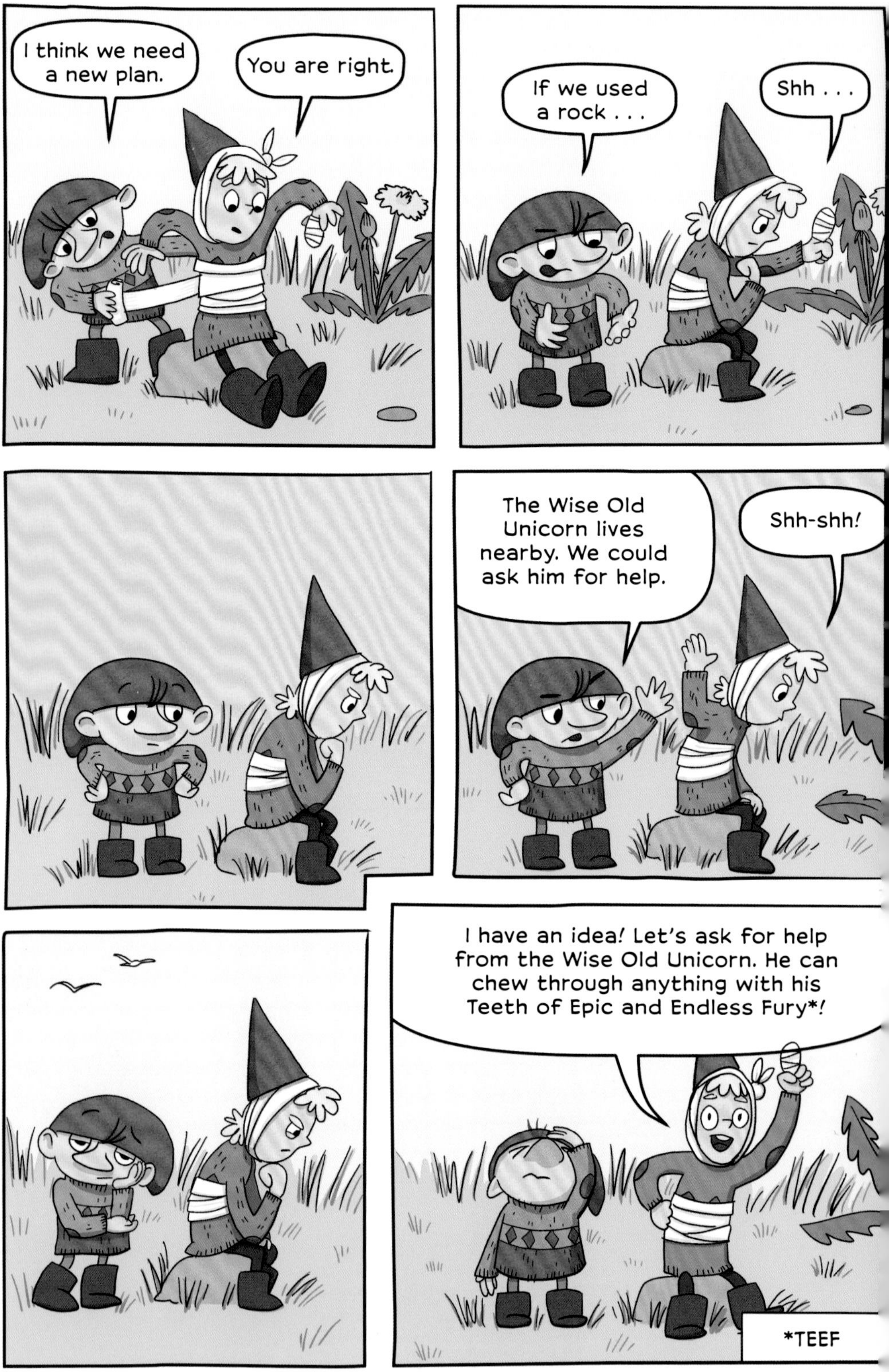
I think we need a new plan.
You are right.
If we used a rock . . .
Shh . . .
The Wise Old Unicorn lives nearby. We could ask him for help.
Shh-shh!
I have an idea! Let's ask for help from the Wise Old Unicorn. He can chew through anything with his Teeth of Epic and Endless Fury*!
*TEEF

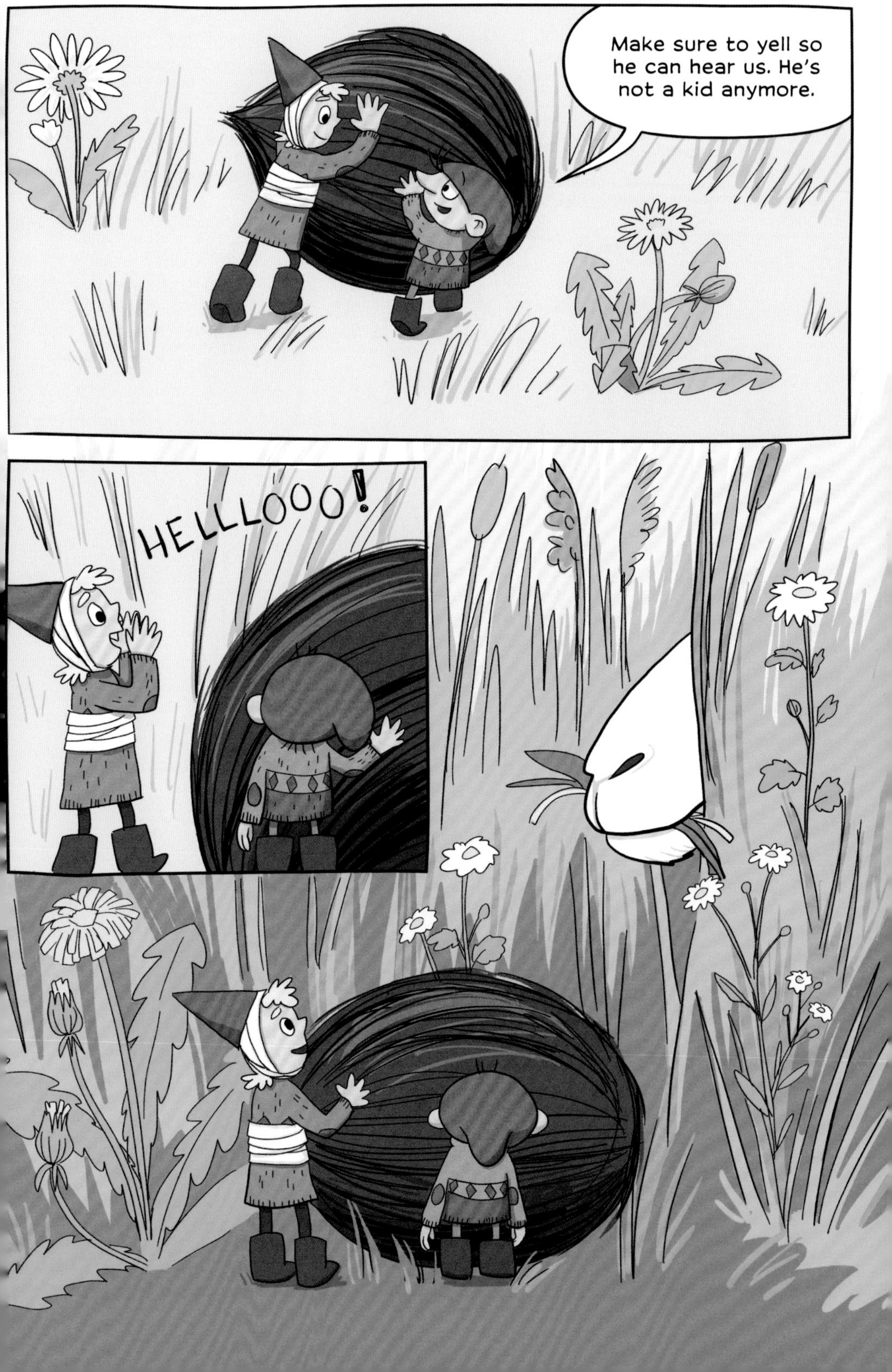

Make sure to yell so he can hear us. He's not a kid anymore.
HELLLOOO!

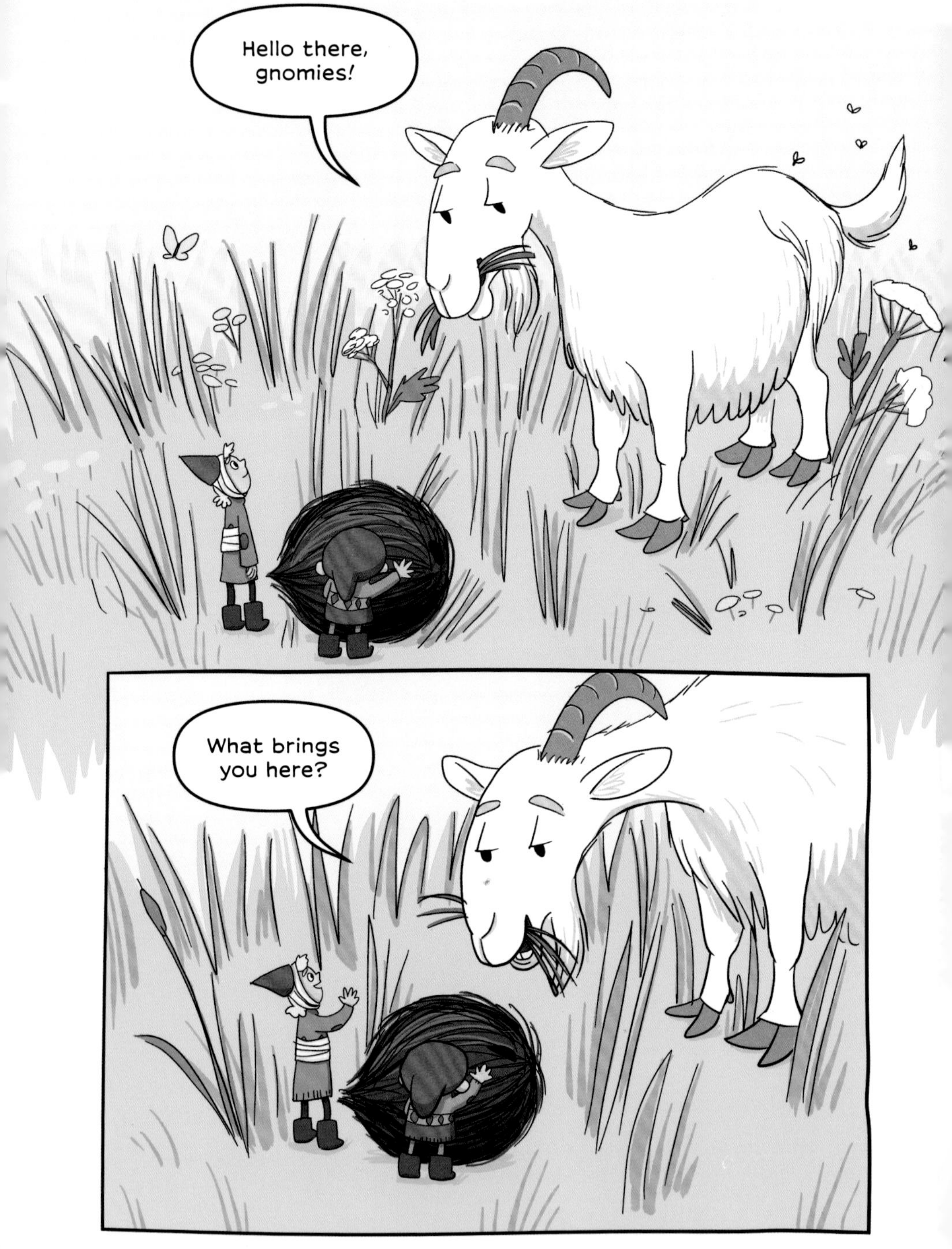
Hello there, gnomies!
What brings you here?

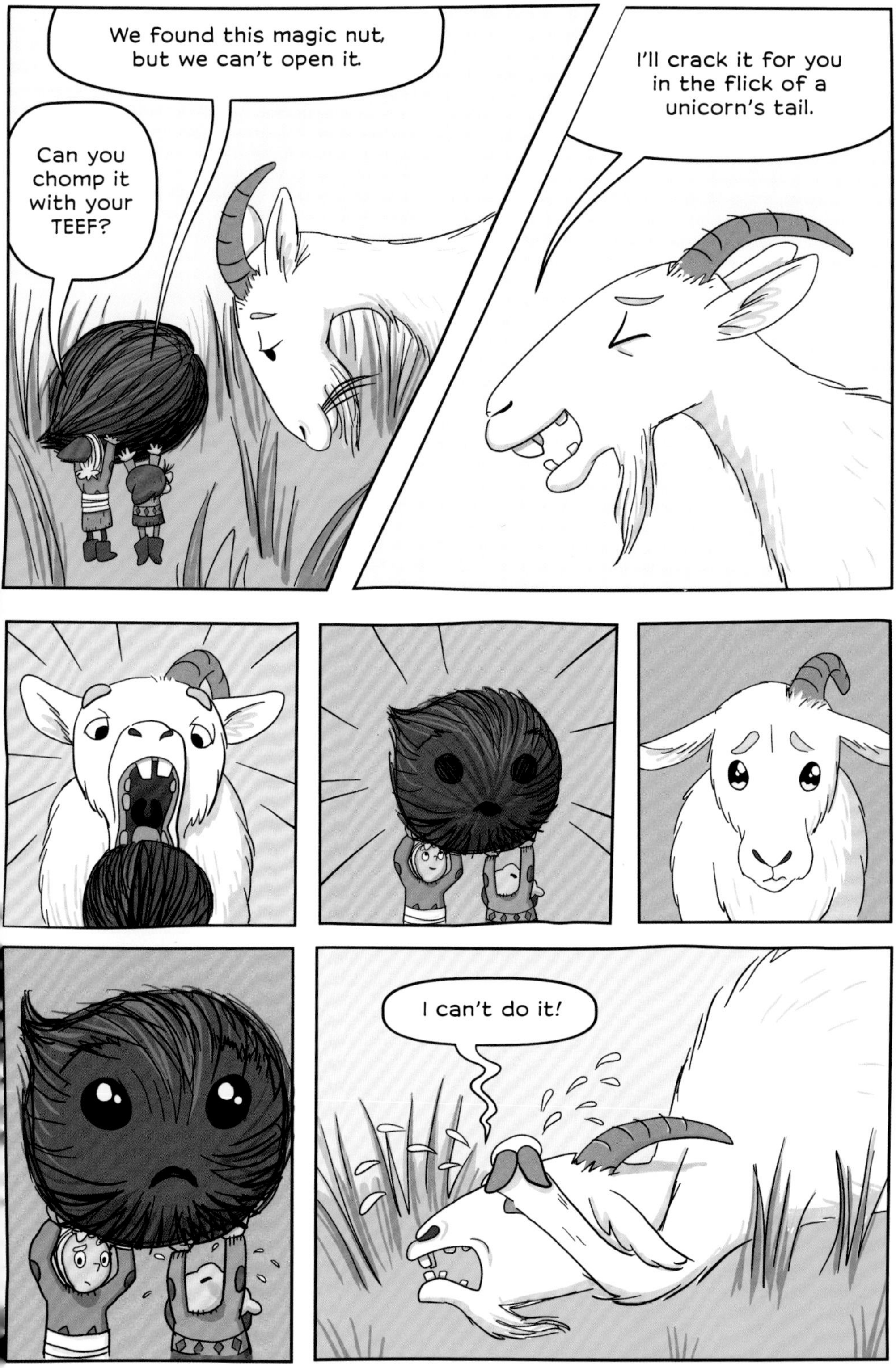
We found this magic nut, but we can't open it.
Can you chomp it with your TEEF?
I'll crack it for you in the flick of a unicorn's tail.
I can't do it!

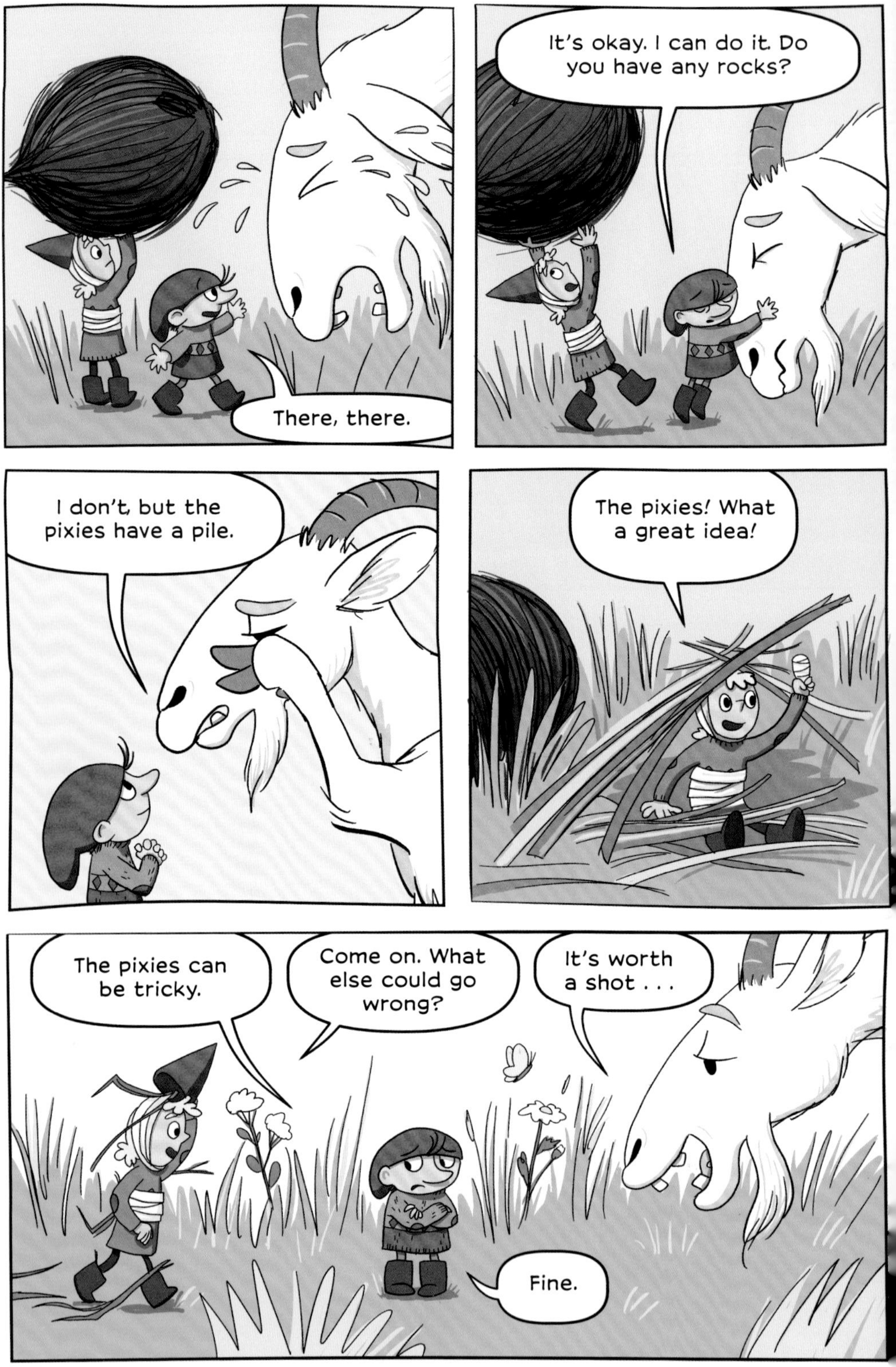
There, there.
It's okay. I can do it. Do you have any rocks?
I don't, but the pixies have a pile.
The pixies! What a great idea!
The pixies can be tricky.
Come on. What else could go wrong?
It's worth a shot . . .
Fine.

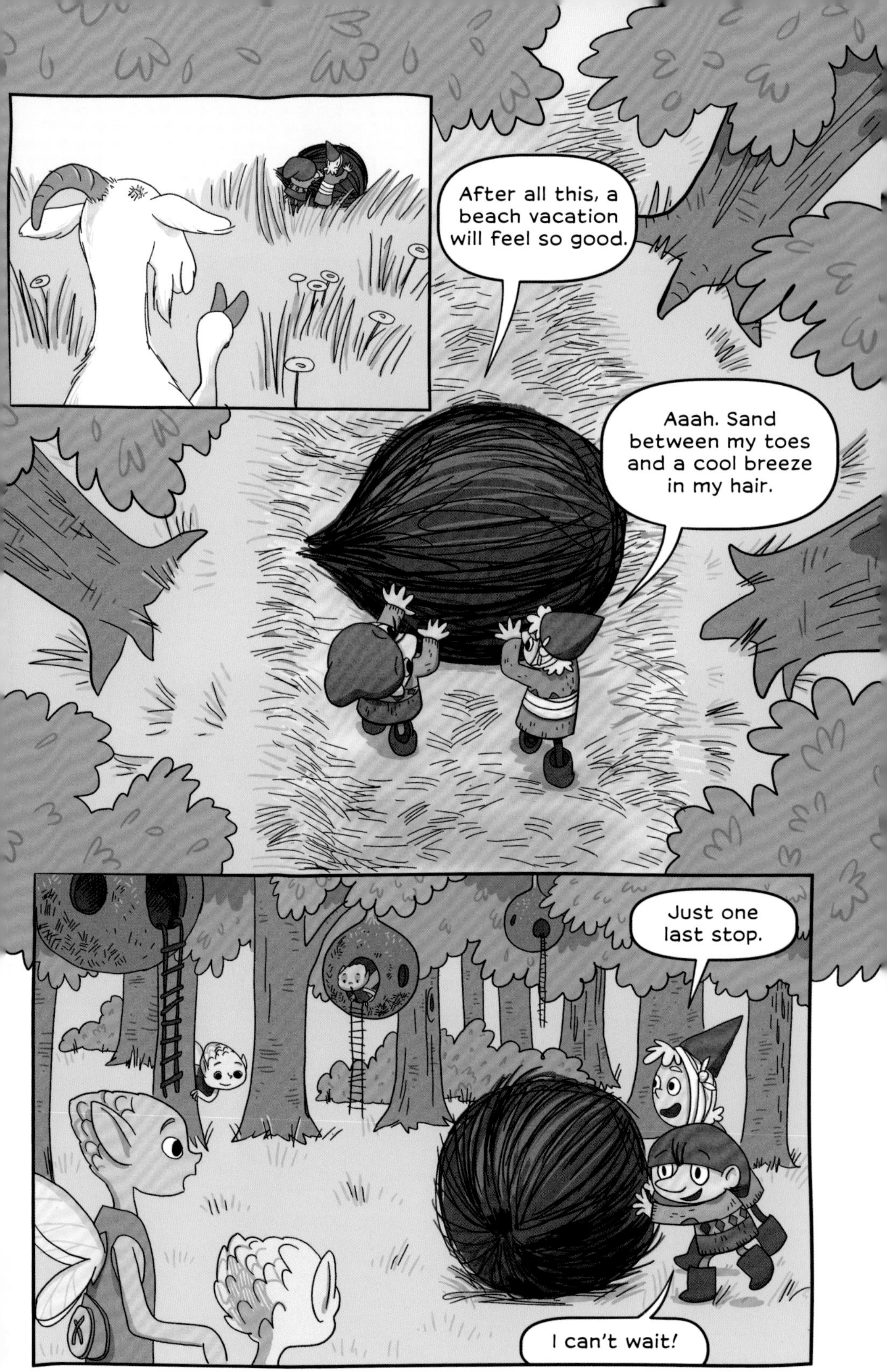
After all this, a beach vacation will feel so good.
Aaah. Sand between my toes and a cool breeze in my hair.
Just one last stop.
I can't wait!

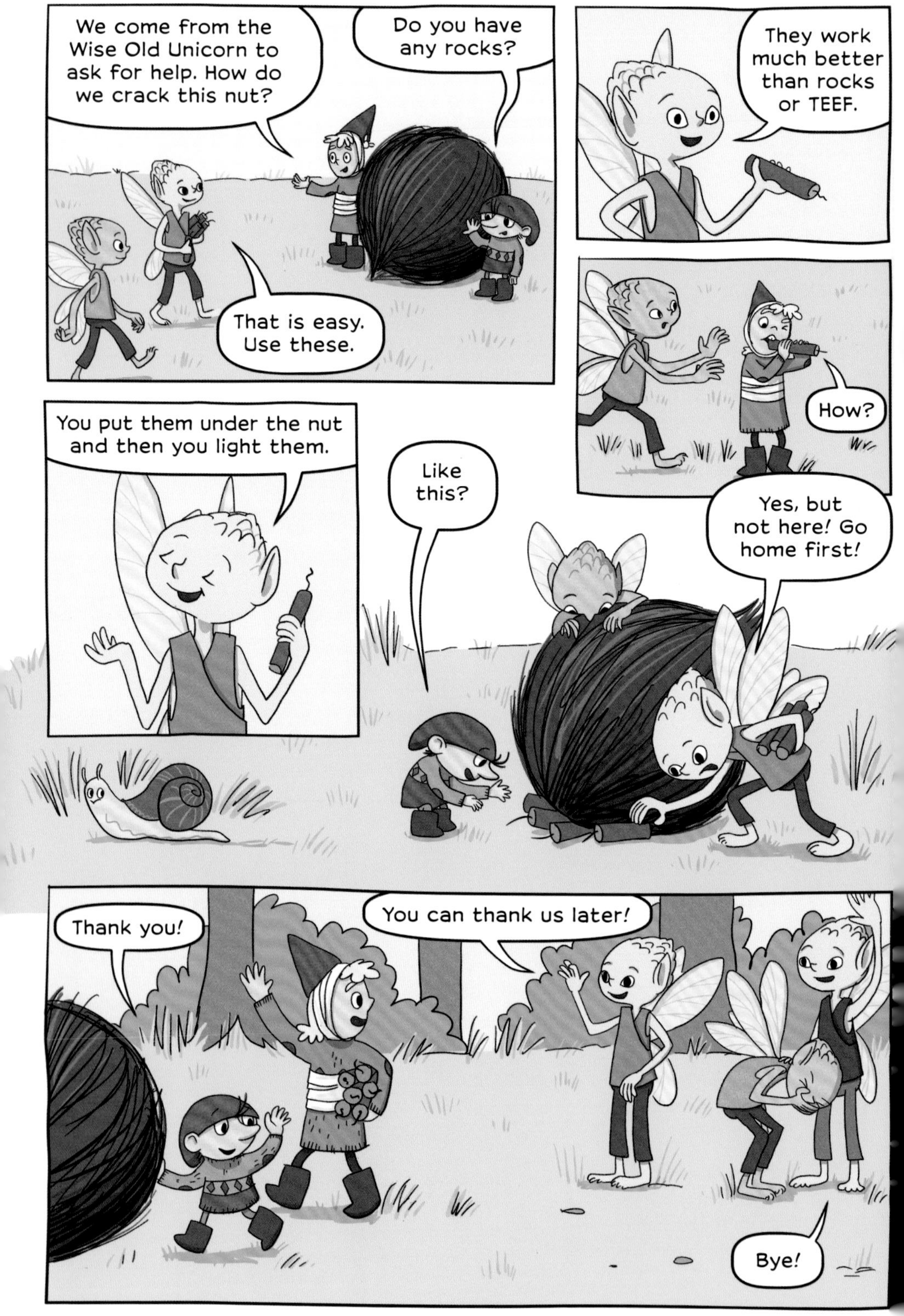

We come from the Wise Old Unicorn to ask for help. How do we crack this nut?
Do you have any rocks?
That is easy. Use these.
They work much better than rocks or TEEF.
How?
You put them under the nut and then you light them.
Like this?
Yes, but not here! Go home first!
Thank you!
You can thank us later!
Bye!

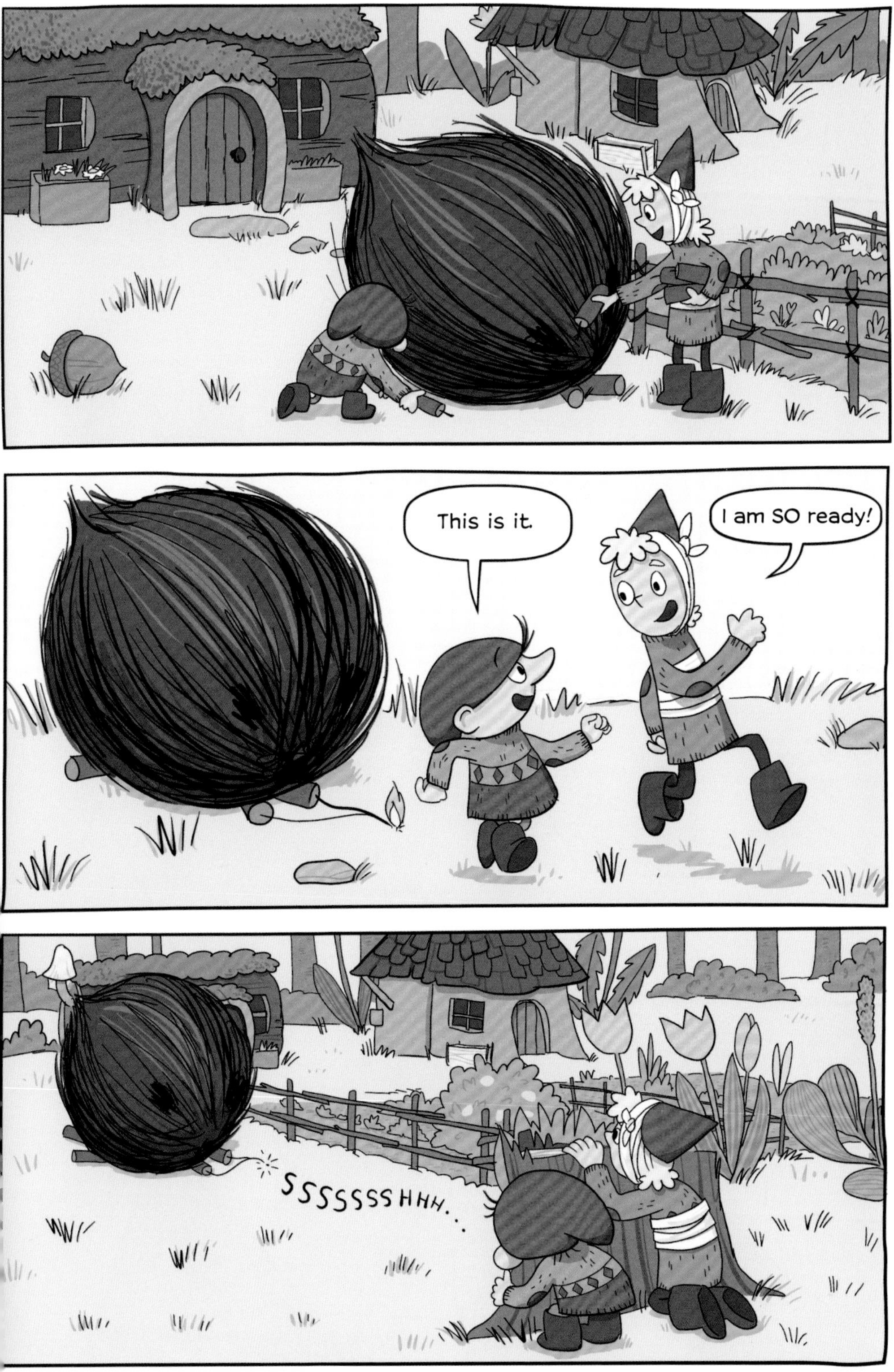
This is it.
I am SO ready!
SSSSSSSHHH...

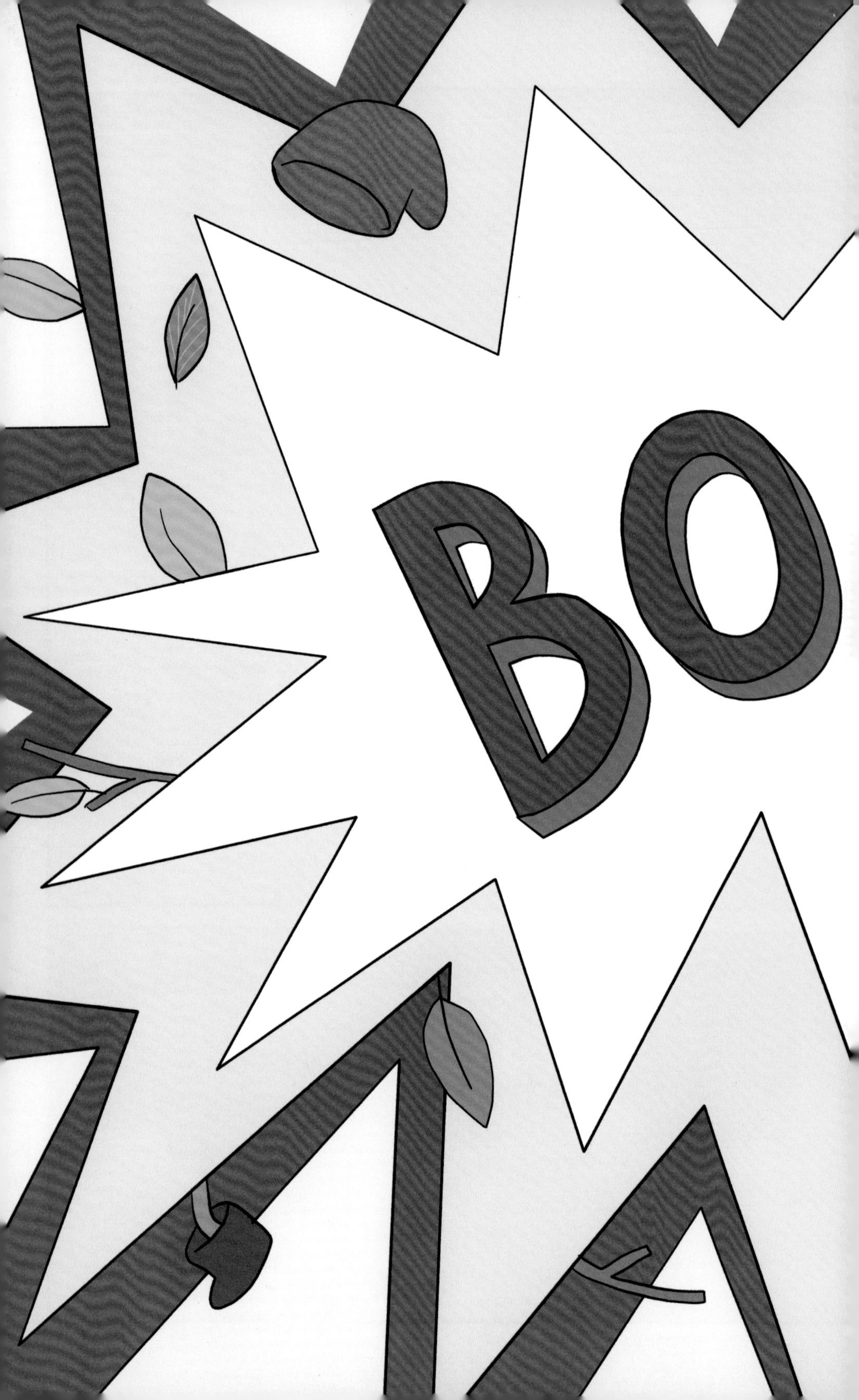
BO

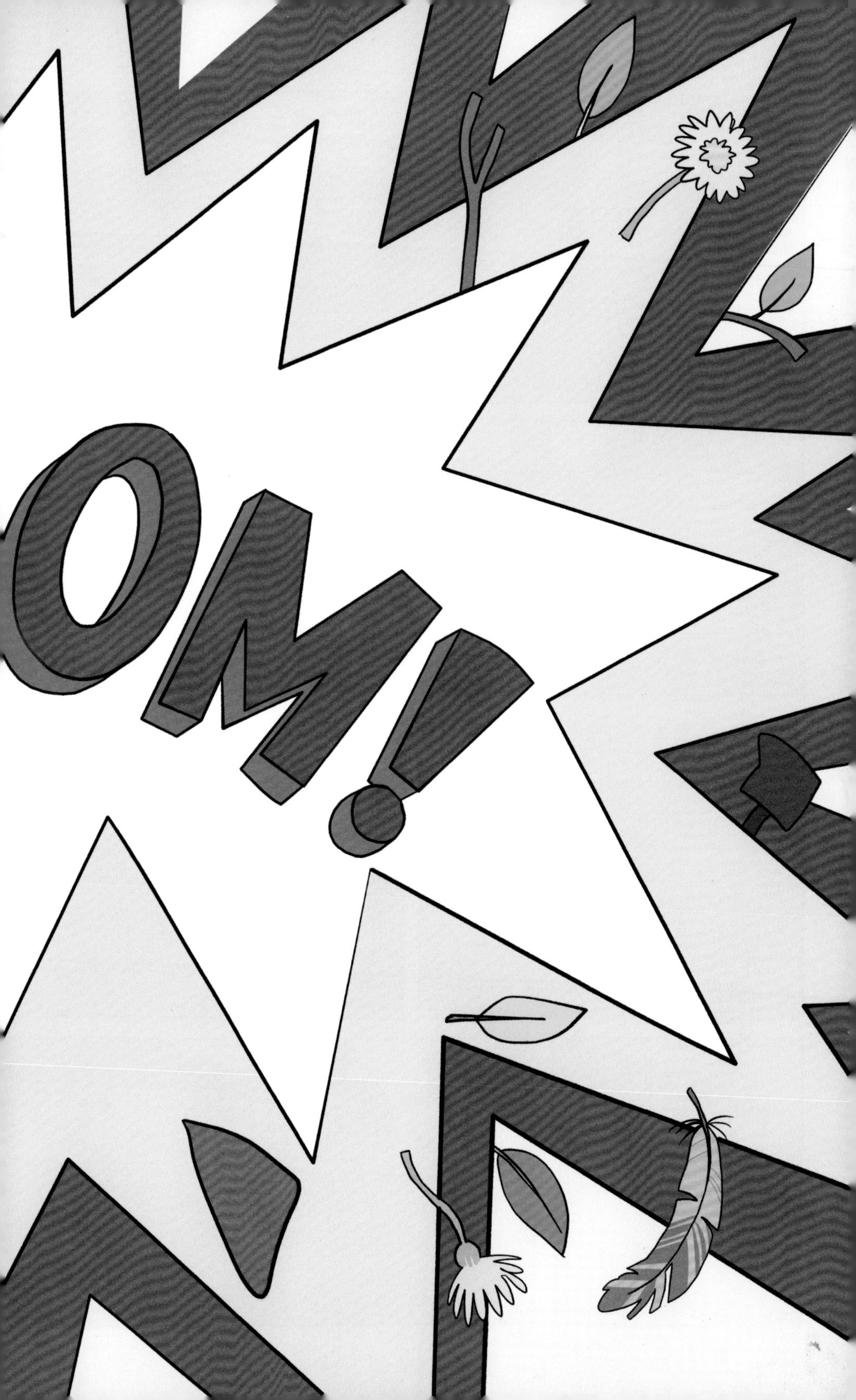
OW!

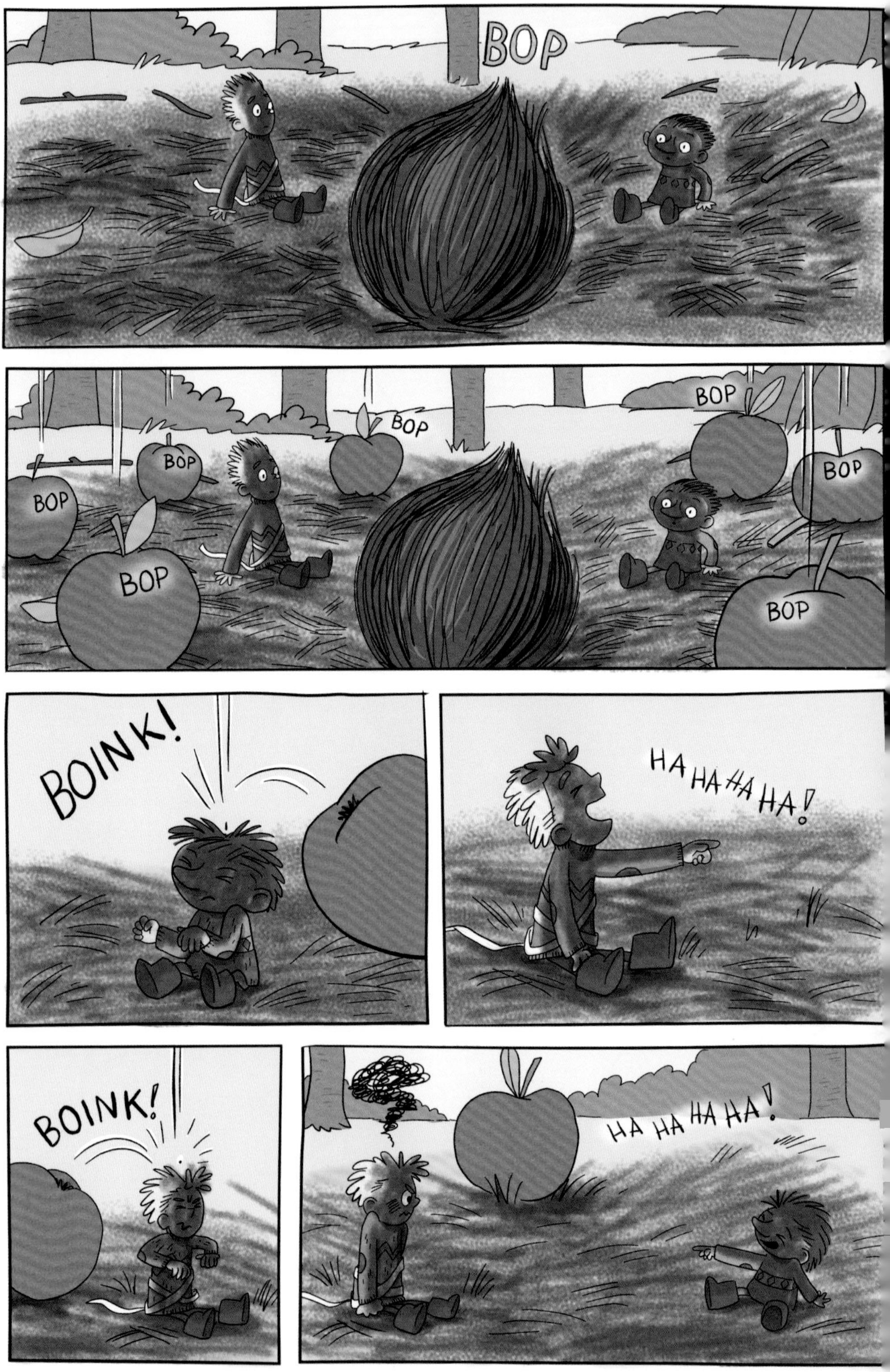
BOP
BOP
BOP
BOP
BOP
BOP
BOP
BOP
BOINK!
HA HA HA HA!
BOINK!
HA HA HA HA!

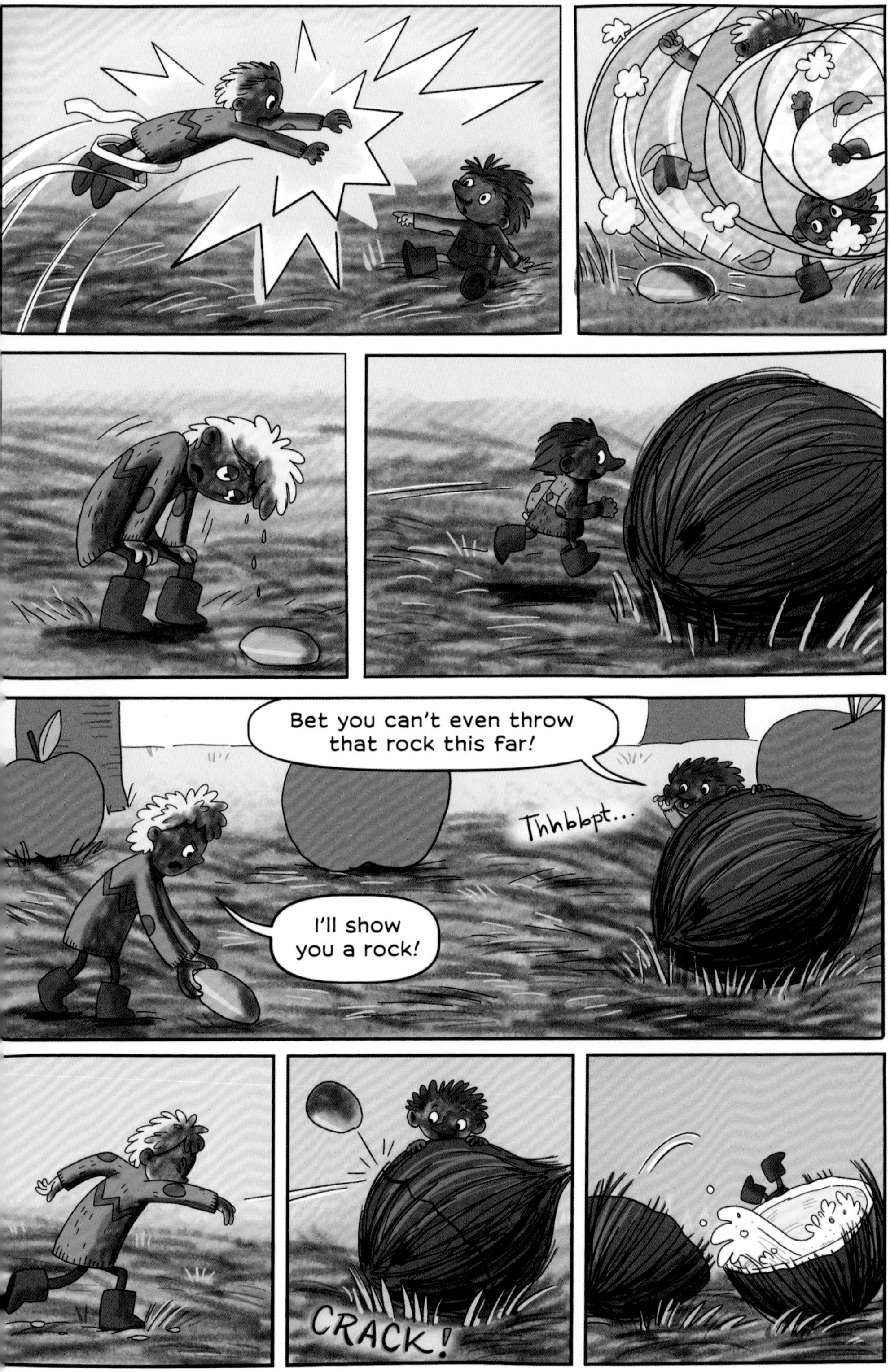
Bet you can't even throw that rock this far!
Thhbbpt...
I'll show you a rock!
CRACK!

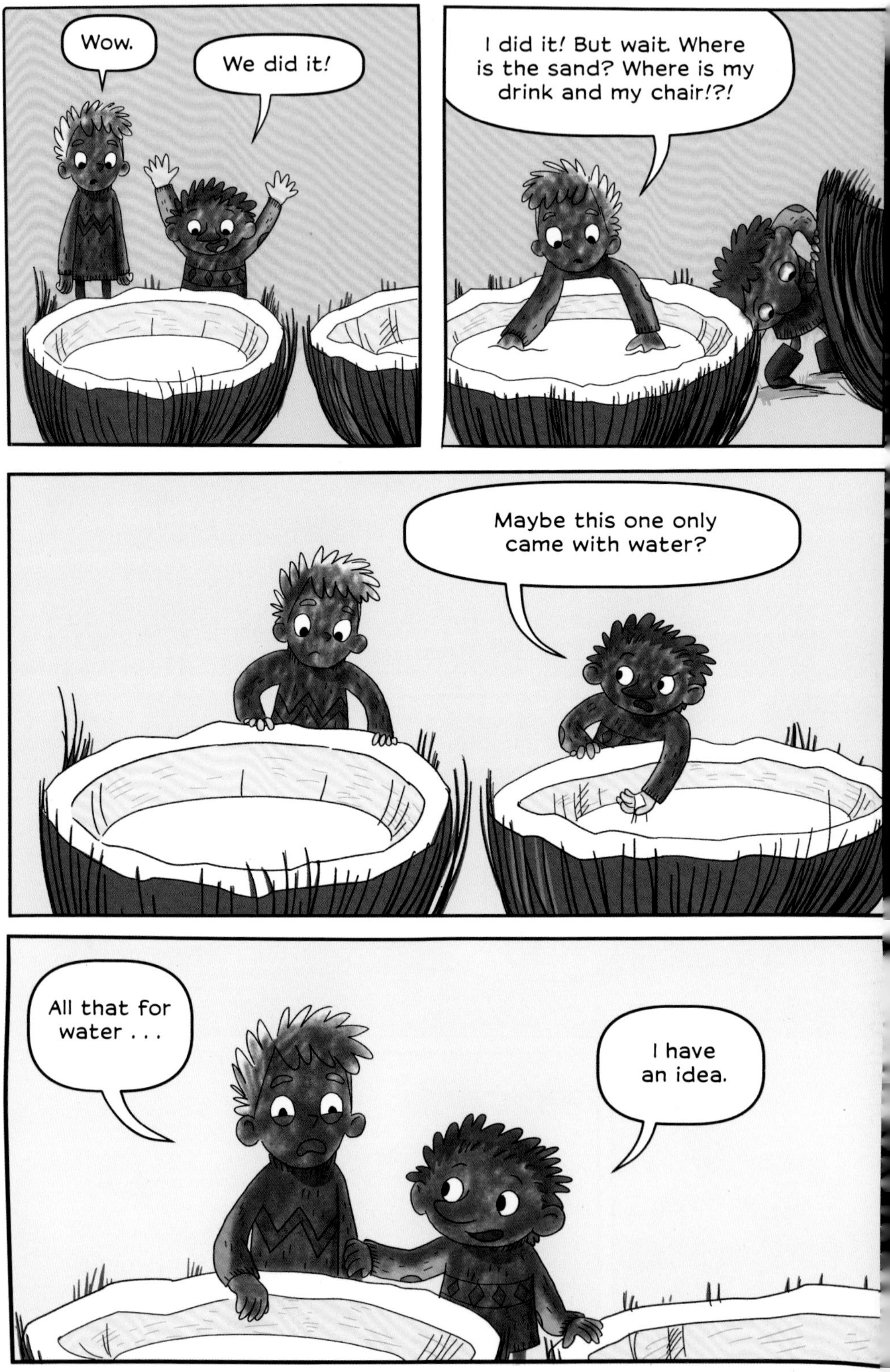
Wow.
We did it!
I did it! But wait. Where is the sand? Where is my drink and my chair!?!
Maybe this one only came with water?
All that for water . . .
I have an idea.